TINSEL TRAUMA

AN ASSEMBLAGE OF HOLIDAY HORROR

NATHAN D. LUDWIG

GENREBLAST
BOOKS

The following stories were previously published:

"Yul Brynner's Yuletide Possession Spectacular" in *The Colour Out of Deathlehem* by Grinning Skull Press

"God Rest Ye Scary Santamen" in *Santa Claws is Coming to Deathlehem* by Grinning Skull Press

"Part & Parcel" in *Twas the Fright Before Christmas in Deathlehem* by Grinning Skull Press

Also available from GenreBlast Books:

The Comfy-Cozy Nihilist: A Handbook of Dark Fiction by Nathan D. Ludwig

Devil Won't Let Me Be by Chad Farmer

Love Potion #666 (second edition) by Nathan D. Ludwig

Midnight Maniacs Volume 1 by Chad Farmer & Nathan D. Ludwig

After Dark in Crazy Town: A Mini-Collection of Dumb Horror by Chad Farmer & Nathan D. Ludwig

Dedicated to every single one of my family members I ever shared a long lost Thanksgiving or Christmas with.

And to those whom I shared either a drink or a kiss on any given New Year's Eve. Or both.

TABLE OF CONTENTS

FOREWORD

When Nathan first approached me about writing an introduction for his new holiday themed collection, I was so excited, I couldn't say, "How much does it pay?" fast enough. Then after actually reading the stories, I waived my five-figure payday and opted to do it for free since I enjoyed them so much.

This is of course bullshit. I was completely floored and quite honored to be asked by him to do this, and I'm still trying to figure out why he thinks anyone would give a damn about what I have to say, but I figure worst case, you can just skip this intro and get right to the good stuff if you're so inclined.

Still here? Alright, just remember, I gave you an out.

I guess I should kick things off by introducing myself. My name is Mike Lombardo. I'm an independent filmmaker, FX artist, and occasional author.*

Now I imagine Nathan made the (foolish) decision to ask me to write this introduction because my debut feature film was a Christmas horror movie. A post-apocalyptic Christmas horror movie in fact, about a mom and her seven-year-old son starving to death in a bomb shelter after the end of the world. Think *The Road* meets *Miracle on 34th Street*. Very bleak, very depressing, and very, very, low budget. *I'm Dreaming of a White Doomsday* is actually how Nathan and I met.

While on the film festival circuit we ran into each other at Crimson Screen Film Festival in South

Carolina where we screened the film. Nathan and Chad Farmer introduced themselves after the screening and cryptically asked me if I was planning on submitting it to GenreBlast Film Festival, which the two of them ran. I read between the lines of the conversation and was quickly (but politely) rebuffed in my offer to head back to their hotel room. As it turns out, they actually really enjoyed the movie and weren't trying to hire my services for the evening.** I did in fact submit *I'm Dreaming of a White Doomsday* to GenreBlast that year and ended up winning Best Feature, but the real prize was getting to know and becoming friends with Nathan and Chad.**** Flash forward seven years and Nathan is a producer and co-writer on my new film, *Dead Format*.

In truth, my connection to Christmas horror goes back much further than *White Doomsday*. I've been obsessed with yuletide terror since I was a very young child. Not even Christmas horror, Christmas in general. People are always shocked to learn that such a diehard extreme horror geek weirdo like me prefers Christmas over Halloween, but that is the case. I love the decorations (especially when people's homes turn into Dario Argento sets from all the colored lights), I love the music, I love the movies (both horror and non) I genuinely just love the vibe of it all. I can be a fairly jaded and cynical person for sure but seeing kids writing letters to Santa and tearing open gifts just warms my heart so much and never fails to make me remember that there used to be magic in my life.

Of course, growing up as a rabid horror fan, my Christmas gifts were almost always purchased by my mom in October. I remember one particularly wonderful year, I put "fake body parts" on my list to Santa, and much to my 10-year-old delight, I opened a mini human abattoir that year under the tree, vowing that I would use all of the severed limbs that my mother had procured from the Halloween store in my first movie. So, you can see that for me, Christmas and horror go together like chocolate and peanut butter.

Another part of the reason I love the holiday so much is just how goddamn bizarre the whole thing is when you look at it from an objective standpoint. An omnipotent obese man who lives in a frozen wasteland spies on children all year judging their behavior and then eventually taking to the skies in a flying sleigh only to break into their homes while they sleep, accepting their offerings of baked goods and animal mammary fluids, and delivering toys bootlegged by an enslaved race of dwarves at his compound.

It's pretty fucking weird right? Of course this is largely due to the mishmash of different cultures, commercial marketing, and the church co-opting the season from the pagans, that all combined to create the Christmas we now know, but it's still a really strange mythology, and it is that strangeness that I think Nathan taps into with these stories so well.*****

You aren't going to find the generic Santa slashers and killer elves here. No, you are about to unwrap a whole slew of bizarre, grotesque, and occasionally cosmic Christmas horrors here, and that's what I loved about the book so much. It felt so different than the usual holiday horror fare (which I still love too) and is one hundred percent Nathan's sensibilities. That might be an indefinable quality if you've never met him or read his work before but trust me when I say it's definitely a thing. Running a giant celebration of obscure genre films from across the world for nearly a decade changes a man.

I don't want to go into detail about the stories themselves as you are about to experience them yourself, and I don't want to spoil anything, but I will say that my personal favorite of the bunch is "Yul Brynner's Yuletide Possession Spectacular". Being a filmmaker and geek, anything involving lost media is sure to pique my interest, especially when the backstory feels as authentic as this, but you really can't go wrong with any of the yuletide fun in this book. All the stories are hilarious, disgusting, nihilistic, and heartwarming all at once.

Just remember, it ain't called *Tinsel Trauma* for nothing.

Mike Lombardo
Lancaster, PA
November 13th, 2024

* - I'm also a shameless self-promotion whore (to be any kind of artist these days you pretty much have to be) so check out my company, Reel Splatter Productions and my short story collection, Please Don't Tap on the Glass and Other Tales of The Melancholy & Grotesque!
** - Remember the part where I said I was a self-promotion whore? Well sometimes in the indie film world, you have to do things you're not particularly

proud of to get your project made, but that's a story for another introduction!***

*** - I am fairly certain that after reading this current introduction, there will likely not be another offer to write anymore introductions, so really soak this one in folks.

**** - And the trophy for winning Best Feature, that was a pretty cool prize too. It sits proudly on my living room mantle alongside a bunch of other trophies we won that year on the festival circuit, a fact that still blows my mind.

***** - You were wondering when I was going to shut the hell up about myself and start talking about the book, weren't you? Well, here you go, and don't forget you CHOSE to keep reading. You could have been halfway through one of the stories right now.******

****** - And don't worry, I'm done with the footnote jokes too. Maybe I was subconsciously trying to make this introduction read like any random page of *House of Leaves*, I don't know.

INTRO

Greetings. Since the effervescent Xmas ghoul known as Mike Lombardo already regaled you with a foreword for the yuletide ages, I'll make this quick.

Why *Tinsel Trauma*? What's that about?

It's simple, dear reader. I can't think of another time of the year when elation and depression comingle so effectively. For every warm memory in your noggin for the end-of-year holidays, there's most likely a cold one lurking as well. For all the presents and food and music that cloud our nostalgia-addled brain, there's also no shortage of loss, pain, regret, and disappointment. Dead relatives and lovers. Loneliness and isolation. The pressure to impress with material things. Watching your figure around all that edible temptation. A veritable minefield of future embedded trauma. With colorful lights wrapped around that trauma lest you forget the good times. For whatever that's worth.

In this collection you'll find some of my favorite kinds of stories all wrapped up in a Winter Solstice bow of darkly comic horror shenanigans. Lost and cursed films, sending up gaudy assembly line Hallmark movies, a heartfelt letter writing session gone horribly wrong, and a madcap combination of the feeling of not having enough of what you need and then the crushing realization of getting more than you had ever bargained for. Love that trope unconditionally.

Everyone loves Halloween horror. What's not to like? It's an easy thing to love. I can smell October just thinking about the 31st and all its increasingly populist trappings. But the real ones out there know that Christmas horror is where it's at. Hiding behind the mistletoe and the tryptophan lurks something truly sinister. It's more than just Krampus and some Gremlins. It's the corruption of youth and innocence. It's broken hopes and shattered dreams. It's getting dumped at your significant other's family home on Thanksgiving. It's experiencing your baby's crib death on the fourth night of Hanukkah. It's getting fired just before Christmas. It's drunk drivers killing people on New Year's. Something so horrible happening around something that's supposed to be so joyous fucks with your brain. Voila. Tinsel Trauma. Halloween ain't got shit on the holidays in the trauma department.

Depressed yet? Well, since you've been so good this year, I've thrown in some bookend stories for good measure. Modest yarns posing as appetizer and dessert, respectively. A peculiar kind of Thanksgiving story starts things off with a flair for the bizarro (only slightly) and then a veritable cutup of a New Year's Eve tale ends things nicely, found footage style. I use the word nicely in the place of a different word like unseemly or impertinent. Just go with it. Make no mistake, though. The real meat of this here book are the four Christmas stories at the heart of it all. Join me in wallowing in all their winter depression glory.

And with that, Happy Thanksgiving, Merry/Happy Christmas, Happy Hanukkah, Happy Kwanzaa, and Happy New Year.

NDL
11/17/24

THE TURKEY TROTS

Mindy and Roderick Galveston had thought about moving Thanksgiving Dinner altogether to Friday nights instead of Thursday permanently for a few years now. It just seemed more practical for them. Who does anything noteworthy on a Thursday anyways? It was pretty much the worst day of the week as far as they were concerned. Tuesday was a close second but at least Tuesday had tacos attached to it if need be. What did Thursdays have? Nothing much since Seinfeld went off the air. Thirsty Thursday? What a vague load of horseshit. If it weren't for Thanksgiving, Thursday would be out on its ass.

It was settled.

If only they were aware of how Dwight D. Eisenhower would feel about the matter.

Such a change of holiday pace would ultimately give them more time to prepare for the 5K Turkey Trot Fun Run they so looked forward to participating in every year on Thanksgiving morning. It was a seasonal staple in the subdivision they had resided in for a decade or so now. Forest Chase Mill. A bastion of middle class stability and secrets. It was a source of pride for Mindy and Roderick to beat the pants off their neighbors in a non-competitive charity event and gloat about it all year thereafter. The Dorn's, a few houses down from them, had recently stepped up their game in the long distance running department and the Galveston's would be damned if their legacy would be usurped by a pair of Johnny-and-Jane-come-latelies. No sir. No ma'am

Besides, moving the big turkey to-do to Friday evening also provided enough time to recover and plan their attack for next year. The dinner itself was merely a side distraction in the way of foot racing glory. It felt more like a nice summation of the week's events when placed on a Friday. The more they thought of it recently, the more it annoyed them that Thanksgiving was somehow on a Thursday or that Thursday even existed to begin with.

The e-vites went out a week beforehand to make it official. "The Galvestons' Friday Thanksgiving Spectacular". Come one, come all to enjoy seasonal finger food and all the gossip one could stand. Sounds delicious, yes? They were banking on the notion of two Thanksgivings in a row would be too much for the suburban gluttons amidst them to resist.

To their elation, nearly everyone invited electronically responded a resounding "yes". The chortling and back-patting that night in the Galveston household was frequent and exuberant. This could start a new trend, Mindy exclaimed. They had to TikTok it, Roderick mused. They'd go viral and be the envy of the neighbors year round, not just on Thanksgiving.

But there was one peculiar RSVP to the shindig that gave them pause. Only a brief one but a pause nonetheless.

The response said:

"I will come but you need to move it back to Thursday, where Thanksgiving belongs. The fourth Thursday of November. Where it unequivocally belongs. Is that understood?"

It was signed a Dwight D. Eisenhower.

"Didn't he lose World War 2? Look that up," Roderick gently demanded.

"I think he was president after that."

"Yeah, during the Great Depression, right? All that socialist stuff, I think."

"Something like that. Tell Gary these email pranks went out of style in 2005."

Gary was Roderick's work friend. He liked Amstel Light and calling women "birds". He said it made him sound cultured. Roderick believed him. Mindy did not believe Roderick when he said such things.

Mindy decided then and there to respond to the email, most likely from Gary, and reply with the following:

"No. Make us change it back."

Thirty-seven minutes later, a reply came while Mindy and Roderick were watching a house flipping show called "Flippin' the Hood". It was not on BET. It was on TruTV and it was painfully white in every way you could imagine it would be.

The response from "Gary" was as such:

"Very well then. I shall. Prepare yourselves and do not say I did not warn you. The sanctity of Thanksgiving on the fourth Thursday of November must be upheld."

-Dwight D. Eisenhower

Under that signature was something new:
    "P.S., I did not lose World War 2. I won that puppy."

Mindy stared at it long and hard with a lemon fart frown on her face.

"What did Gary say? I told him he's not allowed to see your breasts under any circumstances. I did that just for you, babe. I'll tell him again, gimme that thing…"

Roderick looked over the email on Mindy's phone and snorted.

"God. Gary is so stupid. This isn't even funny. I don't get it. Did this Eisenhower guy invent Thanksgiving? Wasn't that the pilgrimages?"

"Pilgrims. And they invented America, Roderick. The Indians invented Thanksgiving by just showing up. Try to keep up."

"Alright, hun. Jeez. Why don't you lay off the daiquiris or you're gonna hurt my feelings real soon, I can taste it."

Mindy snatched her phone back and hastily knocked out another reply.

"We'll be waiting, GARY."

No instant reply came nor did it come five, ten, or fifteen minutes later. Mindy and Roderick went back to their "Flippin' the Neighborhood" mini-binge. Mindy drank another daiquiri. She did not hurt Roderick's feelings as he had feared.

* * *

The reply came while they were asleep. One minute from three in the morning, to be exact.
DING.
Mindy's notification bell went off on her phone along with a throbbing buzz, snapping her out of a dead snore. She grabbed the device and checked it. An email:

"I am in your house. I hope you like music. Also, I am not Gary. He seems nice, though."
-Ike

The smell of brown gravy and jellied cranberry sauce wafted up into their room from downstairs.
Mindy cocked her head at the scent and squinted. Such an email reply would make most people's blood run cold, but then it was followed up with something completely baffling.
"I hope you like music? What kind of response is that? And who the hell is Ike?"
"That's Tina Turner's brother. They banged a lot," Roderick replied with a sleep-addled mumble. Maybe even responding automatically whilst still slumbering.
She whacked him in the arm just to be sure.
"Ow! My feelings!"
He was awake.
"Did you make dinner? What's that smell?"

Before Mindy could reply came the aforementioned music.

Was that "America the Beautiful"? It sounded like it was coming from an old timey radio. Ultra tinny and nigh on grating.

"Oh my god did you leave the Bose Wave Radio on downstairs? And why did you leave it on *that* noise? That thing was quite the deal from Sharper Image I'll have you know."

Roderick was right. It was indeed quite the deal from Sharper Image. But that was in 2005. It was no longer 2005 and Thanksgiving smells and patriotic music from a socialist time machine were currently assaulting their senses in the present year.

"Go check to see what that is."

"What? Why do I have to do that? What about you? Is it because I'm a guy?"

"Yes."

"Paper Rock Scissors."

"No."

"Okay, fine. But you owe me."

"No I don't."

"Alright but I get something for doing this."

"That's basically the same thing as owing you."

"I'm glad we agree. Thank you."

Roderick plugged his nose as he half got out of bed and put one slipper on.

"Ugh. It smells and sounds like America itself morphed into a cat burglar. A really bad one."

"Awesome. Go check just in case it's not."

Roderick made for the hallway with a sigh and a squeaky fart. Mindy checked for another email. Maybe even a text. Nothing.

As Roderick shuffled down the hallway, Mindy could hear him calling out to whoever might be within their abode over the grating patriotic music without a hint of bass whatsoever.

"Come out, come out, wherever you are! Also, I hope you have the instruction manual for that thing. I haven't been able to find it since Obama's second election night."

Roderick's slipper shuffles and voice drifted further away as the music seemed to get louder and louder. It went on for what felt like minutes upon minutes as Mindy sat there covering her ears tightly. And then just as it all started, it went away. Gone was the music and gone were the seasonal scents. Poof.

Mindy sat in drowning silence, relieved but also quite unnerved. She couldn't hear anything at all including Roderick. A vacuum of noise. She worried aloud if she might have gone deaf.

"Have I gone deaf?"

She hadn't gone deaf, no. But it was hard for her to tell with such an absence of sound.

DING.

Mindy checked her phone. A text this time. Upgrading, are we?

The text simply stated:

"Change it back to Thursday or Roderick gets it."
-Ike

Mindy frowned as she quickly replied with:

"Gets what?"

About a minute went by. Then:

"Seriously? I have to explain this?"
-Ike

Mindy decided to choose her words carefully but felt it necessary to inform this Ike of something extremely important:

"Yes. Also, you don't have to sign your name to a text. I figured it was you. Whover you are."

Ten seconds later:

"IT'S DWIGHT D. EISENHOWER. IKE IS MY NICKNAME. THERE'S NO WAY YOU'RE THAT STUPID. IT'S IMPOSSIBLE."
-IKE

She mouthed her next reply out loud as she responded:

"All caps is way out of pocket. You really should check that next time you hit send. It gives off super negative vibes."

A reply came supernaturally fast. Like two seconds later. Like he didn't even fully read her reply. She was more than a little hurt at such a perceived slight.

"Change your Thanksgiving dinner back to Thursday or Roderick will have something awful happen to him. Is that better? Easier to understand?"

What was this Ike going to do to her Roddy? Kill him? Really? That seemed a little dramatic to her. So she replied thusly:

"Like what? You have to be more specific."

Minutes went by and the texts stopped altogether. She waited a full fifteen minutes before attempting another reply:

"…Hello?"

Instead of a text, something sounded out from somewhere downstairs. A low, booming singing? Was that coming from Roderick?

"…He is trampling out the vintage where the grapes of wrath are stored…"

"…Uh, Roderick? Baby?"

Footsteps were echoing up the stairs as the booming voice continued…

"He hath loosed the fateful lightning of His terrible swift sword…"

Mindy frantically dialed 911 as the voice filled the hallway, about to burst through the room in mere seconds.

"…His truth is marching on…"

No signal now for some reason.

"…What? The hell?"

Roderick stomped into the room, the source of the bassy musicality. He made for Mindy on the bed with a wicked, toothy grin as he continued, swinging his arms like he was in some kind of marching band from Hell.

"Glory, glory, hallelujah!"

"Roddy? Baby? What are you doing?"

"Glory, glory, hallelujah!"

Mindy backed away as much as she could, right to the edge of the far side of the bed. Near to falling right off.

"Glory, glory, hallelujah!"

"Roddy! Stop this right now! This is not sexy at all!"

"His truth is marching on!"

Mindy screamed as Roddy crawled onto the bed, that same toothy grin planted on his face. He had stopped singing though and cocked his head as he observed Mindy like he was seeing her in the flesh for the first time. Too scared to move, Mindy chanced a question.

"…Roddy?"

Nothing. Just that awful smile-stare.

Mindy gulped.

"…Ike? Is… Is that you"

And then Roddy spoke in a voice that was most certainly not his own. It sounded like some old guy. Some old guy from the Great Depression. Or World War 2. Or both.

"Hi Mindy! Have you changed your mind yet? I was quite serious about the sanctity of keeping Thanksgiving on the fourth Thursday of November.

As President of the United States, it's my duty to uphold a storied tradition set for by God himself, Abraham Lincoln. Surely you understand when it's put that way, young lady. Am I right?"

"What did you do to Roddy? Why does he sound like a Ben Gay TikTok ad from the 1980s?"

Ignoring her question altogether, Roddy lunged for her and grabbed her by the shoulders as she squealed in terror. Roddy's mouth opened wide and that voice came out again but this time without the need for the movement of a mouth at all. Roddy's speaking space looked like an uncovered manhole as the voice emanated from it like a radio broadcast.

"Through Thanksgiving, Americans should celebrate the plentiful yield of our soil. The beauty of our land. The preservation of those ideals of liberty and justice that form the basis of our national life, and the hope of international peace."

As he spoke, something flowed out of Roddy's mouth. A green, glowing essence of some sort. It then flowed straight into Mindy's mouth as she screamed again. Her screams turn to gags and gurgles as the ghostly substance that looked a lot like the thirty-fourth President of the United States of America, complete with bad combover and lit cigarette wormed its way into her orally.

"Let us be grateful that the foundations of freedom in our Nation grow stronger with each passing year, giving hope to fettered peoples that they may walk as free men unafraid; that the yield of our soil and the production of our factories have been abundant, enriching our lives and enabling

us to share our bounty with less fortunate ones in other lands; and that the forces of nature are being harnessed for peaceful purposes, bringing limitless possibilities of comfort and happiness both to ourselves and to future generations. This I proclaim. Happy Thanksgiving to all!"

As Ike or whatever the thing was finished transferring itself into Mindy, Roddy began warbling madly like a giant turkey on some sort of illegal stimulant or two.

Mindy gagged some more and then grabbed her phone instinctively.

"Well then. Looks like we're gonna have to reschedule Thanksgiving from Friday to Thursday. I think everyone will be okay with that. What do you think, babe? I'll re-do the invites. I'm sure Gary will be pissed but fuck him. Right?"

"Gobblegobblegobblegobblegobblegobblegobblegob blegobblegobblegobble..."

"I'm glad we agree, sweetie. Thanks, Ike. You saved Thanksgiving for us and for all of America."

Mindy reached into her mouth with her free hand and pulled out a pack of unfiltered Camel Reds and a pack of matches from a bar called the Loosey Goosey in Poughkeepsie, New York. She lit a match and ignited the cigarette with a couple puffs.

Ike's voice boomed out of her mouth again as she braced herself on the bed.

"You're a good egg, Mindy Galveston. Proclamation 3163 remains intact. God bless America."

Mindy looked down at her lit cig and then looked at a gobbling Roderick, who was now smacking his head into the wall as the drywall and plaster dented and cracked and blood pit-patted onto his face in small smears. Feathers burst through his skin as his warble-gobbles intensified into a hysterical crescendo.

Mindy looked quizzically at Roderick then at her cigarette in the same manner.

"Hoo boy. I gotta quit these things cold turkey."

Yul Brynner's Yuletide Possession Spectacular

So how many lost and/or unfinished films do you think are really out there? I mean the ones that no one knows even exist. Think about it. All those nuclear warheads that went unaccounted for after the collapse of the Soviet Union. Scary, right? Now just think about how many weird, bizarre, and uncouth films never saw the light of day. Productions that would make *Manos: The Hands of Fate* look like *Follow That Bird* in comparison. Years become decades; the crew gets older and older. They don't tell the right people about any of their experiences so as a result, when they die, nothing gets passed on. No clickbait article, no glib hipster critic mini-doc. Nothing. Just the sheer volume of films that were actually finished and released and are now lost to time and poor storage habits alone boggles the mind.

But I find myself thinking more about the lost ones. Unfinished. Unreleased. Unseen.

How? Why?

The *why* really keeps me awake at night.

At this point, it would be decidedly redundant to say that most people think Hollywood screen legend Yul Brynner retired from feature films in 1976. *Futureworld* and *Death Rage* rounded out his career. Not exactly a golden-charioted sendoff but hardly a trapdoor chute into a landfill, either. That's the common knowledge take of it all, at least. However, if you are like me and enjoy pulling a magnifying glass up to the cracks of someone's acting career, you'll find all kinds of interesting things. And if you make your intentions known in certain circles, you'll get all kinds of interesting *people* jockeying for your attention. It happened to me almost as if in a dream.

And that is what I'm most anxious to tell you about. I'm not so worried that you won't believe me. I'm more concerned that you *will*. This odd profession has no more room for the curious. It's now just filled with people like me, wishing they could unsee what cannot be unseen under any circumstances. Not even in death. At least, that's what I'm told.
So in lieu of that, I must tell you what I know about Yul Brynner's unfinished Christmas horror film.

The Demon of Noel Crossing.

Ridiculous, right? Maybe not so much as you might think. If you tell me you've heard of it, I will call you a liar and this exchange will cease faster than it commenced.

Good. Good. That's a good answer. We can continue.

Now then, if you're ready, I will tell you all I know about Mr. Brynner's shuttered film role as it was told to me. You'll forgive me if I ramble a few times here or there or the pitch of my voice changes ever so slightly. It's a recent malady I am still coming to terms with. Apologies in advance.

I'm not even going to ask you if you've ever heard of D.R. Ford, because I know you haven't. Nevertheless, he was quite a prolific director and producer in the 60s and 70s even though none of his films ever saw the light of day. Some films were finished, wet prints and all, and some never made it through principal photography. There are stories of all kinds floating about if you really want to look hard enough. I won't waste your time on most of them as they are for those with hardier stomachs than you or I. Just know that most of them weren't released for good reason.

The one that never gets talked about is D.R. Ford's planned Christmas horror film that he was dead set on shooting around and during the actual holiday. Occasion-themed horror films were a scarcity in the 70s and to actually shoot it on the corresponding holiday? The unions would be apoplectic. That's why the ever-intrepid DRF decided to go non-union and shoot it as a completely independent production. His pockets were deep and so little was known about him or his background, that no one could come up with the right questions to ask about where the money was coming from or why he insisted on shooting on actual Christmas of all times. He had zero intentions of skimping on the budget just because he circumvented the influence of the union. Oh no. Top of the line cast and crew. In fact, a few sources over the years were adamant he spent more on the production as an independent film than he probably would have through the normal cogs and whistles of the grand ol' Hollywood machine.

The usual suspects were insisted upon. Donald Pleasance. James Mason. Vincent Price. Christopher Lee. Peter Cushing. Ford sneered at every recommendation. He knew who he wanted. Yul Brynner. A titan of Hollywood whose star had faded a smidge, occasionally leading him to the genre watering hole of spaghetti westerns and Italian crime films. His hold on the role of King Mongkut in the never-ending stage revivals of *The King and I* meant D.R. Ford had to time it just right if he were to snag his dream leading man for the role of Father Simeon.

Yes, that's right. Father Remus Simeon. After all, *The Demon of Noel Crossing* was a movie about a Catholic priest performing an exorcism on himself during a return to his hometown for Christmas. At least, that was the plot on the surface.

I've spoken to several sources. Exhausted sources of sources, even. Every single one of them confirmed to me that what was really going on was some form of summoning ceremony disguised as a film shoot. DRF was adamant about Brynner joining their fold, whatever their fold *was* exactly was never made crystal clear to me. I ended up finding that out all on my own. Lucky me.

While Yul Brynner's last theatrical film, *Death Rage*, was in theaters in the brisk Autumn of 1976, D.R. Ford made his play for Brynner to be in his ambitious horror film. I mean, if you really think about, Yul Brynner as a stoic Catholic priest fighting to vanquish the evil inside of him during Christmas sounds like an amazing film. Potentially amazing, of course.

Too bad it was all a lie.

Money was thrown around. Lots of money. More money than was normally bandied about for a leading man in any size film at the time. I believe that's partly why it was never printed in the trades. It was a number so large that everyone from Variety to The Hollywood Reporter balked and thought it to be a practical joke or a publicity stunt. Brynner was convinced to postpone preparations to reprise his famous role in *The King and*

I briefly so he could travel to Bumpass, Virginia to star in his first horror film. Folks surrounding him apparently convinced the legend that it could be his *The Exorcist* and launch him back into the limelight. It worked, regardless of sincerity or accuracy.

I've spoken to most of the crew of the film over the years. Most of them. Some I've heard their account secondhand long after their death. A lot of them were part of the old Hollywood system and were already on borrowed time. Others were young and eager beavers, high on the current studio system of cutting-edge method acting and narrative experimentalism. It was an odd melding of cultures and personalities. The ones still left alive won't talk to me anymore. They tell me it's bad for them and too late to do anything for me. Whatever that means.

There was cinematographer Lucio Gonzetti. A veteran cameraman of Italian crime and action films for decades. This was his first gig as DP and to say he was more than a little amped about it would be a gross understatement.

Makeup and special effects artist Maria Fancher was one of the bright-eyed young ones. Originally a stage makeup artist out of New England, she packed up everything and moved to L.A. in a last-ditch attempt to make something of a career in film even though becoming a successful movie makeup artist as a woman back then was less likely than pulling an actual makeup kit out of your own ass. It wasn't impossible per se, but highly unlikely.

D.R. Ford's right-hand man was the screenwriter himself, Nick Simon. They were seemingly inseparable and from all accounts shared the same mind. It sounds cute as an expression, but after all my research I think they actually *were* the same mind. No one can seem to contact Simon. Not even my deep cover contacts. The ones who never reveal their names.

When I finally got around to asking one of my sources why DRF insisted on shooting the film *on* Christmas, I was told matter-of-factly that the pagans who originally celebrated the holiday that was eventually bastardized and re-branded as a Christian holiday knew that that time of year was attuned to a specific doorway that could only be opened on or as close to the day as possible.

What doorway? I had to ask.

The one to the abyss. That was their answer.

That particular source of mine was a lost films crusader known only as PenitentOne on the dark web.

They stopped responding to my emails after that.

To say my contacts were dwindling at that point would be a bit of an exaggeration. They weren't exactly growing, either. I knew I had a few sources that would stick with me to the end, if only for them to know that I now see what they see. Camaraderie, if you will. If there can be such a thing when it comes to…

…Hold on. I'll be right back.

* * *

Huh. Funny. I could have sworn I heard someone in my front room. Then when I was in my front room, I was certain I heard someone in here. In my study. With you. Are you sure you didn't hear anything unusual? Very well. I'll take your word for it.

Now where was I? My contacts? Ah yes, they were a most motley variety of former crewmembers and urban legend investigators. A few journalists in there for good measure and some unconfirmed reports of actual cast members. I felt like had a proper handle on the breadth of information and opinions that were out there. It helped me form my own ideas and theories of what really happened on that film set.

I knew I had to make a documentary out of all this. Why had no one else thought of it yet?
Maybe they had. Maybe there was a reason one never materialized. I panicked. What if everyone who was still alive had already been interviewed by some hack vlogger and now the window had closed for the chance at a true account of this storied cinematic debacle?

I made my intentions known in the circles I frequented online. Both in the legal and illegal realms. Shortly afterwards, I was contacted by my last and best source on the film. Known simply as modranicht76, they seemed to know almost everything about the shoot. Pre-production, principal photography, how it all ended, the aftermath, the works.

It was astonishing. It was frightening.

I asked my other contacts about this modranicht76 and the validity of their claims. Some warned me to stop talking to them. Others ghosted me completely. Jealousy? Competitive passive-aggression? Maybe it was one of them playing a prank on me. Goading me into going whole hog on a boondoggle of a documentary they knew would end up in wild goose territory.

Looking back on it all, I wish any or all of those notions were indeed true. The lure of the perfect urban legend-meets-reality documentary was too strong for me to resist. I had to know it all. My encounters with modranicht76 usually began in the dark early hours of morning, between one and three, and lasted until the peeking rays of dawn. For days on end.

Through it all, I couldn't glean one single shred of information on who exactly modranicht76 was. D.R. Ford? Nick Simon? I became so obsessed and tuned in to my conversations with them that in fleeting moments I almost convinced myself it was Yul Brynner himself.

It's insane, I know. But you really need to know how strong the lure of this whole thing was for me. This was the Mount Everest of lost films and the motherlode when it came to obscure urban legends. The Roanoke Island or the Ourang Medan of the film world. Some film historians or critics won't even carry on a conversation with you if you so much as hint at mentioning *The Demon of Noel Crossing*. One of Yul Brynner's biographers and even his own son, Rock, refused to believe any inkling of the film being real. No one seems to remember the director or screenwriter even existing in the first place. Except in my circles. The hidden circles you won't find mentioned on Reddit or 4chan.

There are pictures.

I've *seen* them.

Pictures of the chapel they built on the outskirts of Bumpass. Pictures of Yul Brynner smiling on set. Pictures of Yul Brynner not smiling on set. Pictures of Yul Brynner looking at someone just offset out of the corner of his eye.

Some*thing*.

And pictures of the fire. The fire that destroyed the church set and killed thirteen members of the cast and crew.

Oh. You didn't hear about that part in the papers, did you?

Neither did anyone else for that matter. It effectively ended the shoot for good. The surviving cast and crew were compensated for their time, the town of Bumpass was paid for any damages incurred and D.R. Ford and Nick Simon faded from the narrative. From *any* narrative for that matter. There are no more mentions even in the most labyrinthine of investigative circles of DRF, Simon, or any future projects they might have tried to shepherd into existence.

They were just gone. Done. Poof.

A few intrepid researchers tried to look for DRF and Simon. One we know of never returned from their travels. Another did, but soon went completely insane. You can visit them at the Piedmont Psychiatric Institute, but make sure you don't bring anything sharp or have an affinity for uninterrupted sleep without any nightmares. I chose to forego a visit and take that particular source's word for it.

The theory still persists to this day that DRF and Simon were (are?) the same person. No one interviewed in any capacity ever recalled seeing Ford and Simon in the same room or sometimes even seeing Simon at all in the flesh. Was he a conjuring of DRF's design? A split personality created to deal with the glorious burden of being a visionary screenwriter?

Though hide nor hair has ever been found of D.R. Ford or Mr. Simon, one other thing was indeed found.

The film itself.

I have yet to see it, but a whole reel of dailies for *The Demon of Noel Crossing* surfaced about fifteen years ago in the National Archives at Mount Pony in Culpeper, Virginia. Just an hour away from Bumpass.

All reports (about five) of the footage seem to purport that Yul Brynner was giving an all-time performance as the tortured priest battling possession deep within his soul on Christmas of all holidays. One source said it was like *It's a Wonderful Life* meets *The Verdict* with *The Exorcist* thrown in for good measure. I envy the eyes that laid their gaze on such a rare find. I think that's why Brynner seemed so crestfallen in certain interviews for his latest run on *The King and I* following the failed film that no one would ever know about.

I think something out there appreciated his performance. And still does. *They* fed off of it, after all. Doorways don't open themselves, you know.

You've probably been thinking this whole time one prevailing thought. One nagging notion that won't go away.

Why Yul Brynner? What's the connection?

Well, I'm sure you're expecting some eleventh-hour tie-in that links everything together. The lynchpin in the whole sordid story that gives us all that much sought after "aha" moment.

I'm sorry to say that there isn't one.

Except for the fact that D.R. Ford was a collector of actors. No. Movie stars. Hollywood legends.

I can't be one hundred percent certain, but from many of the accounts and conversations I've had over these long handful of years, whoever or whatever is truly behind Ford and Simon and their odd productions gains power from high celebrity status. The adoration of fans, the sheer skill and charisma involved in being a bankable movie star has a cosmic commodity, apparently.

I know what you're thinking. *What?*

Before Brynner they tried it with William Holden, of all people. DRF was all set to direct a tropical horror thriller called *Savage Solstice* in 1970 starring Mr. Holden as a professor of anthropology searching for a missing link troglodyte terrorizing a coastal town in Argentina. Sensing a pattern here? Horror films shooting in out-of-the-way locations and starring big name movie stars. All for what?

Well, look at the filming dates. Summer Solstice. Winter Solstice.

Are you getting it yet?

The Solstice and Equinox days on our calendar are a veritable Russian roulette of dimensional doorways if you know how to open them. Kill a bunch of people at the right time and wait for said door to swing wide just for you.

The shoot for *Savage Solstice* ended abruptly when the second unit camera crew drowned during a freak tropical storm. Twelve dead in all. Cameramen, stunt divers, production assistants. All lost to the depths.

It became pretty clear after I found out this bit of info what was really going on. No one had any intention of finishing these films. They were all a ruse to set up a sacrifice in order to open a portal to an abyss long forgotten by mortal memories. I check and I checked and I could not find any proof of any odd horror film shoots occurring on any Equinox during the last sixty years. I called on my ever-reliable sources, hoping and praying they would come up with the same goose eggs that I had in my latest searches.

Instead…

1949. Fay Wray was set to star in the noir chiller *The Man with The Silver Hands* near Thunder Bay, Ontario.

I think you know where this is going by now. I wanted to pretend it was all a dream when I heard what had happened. A twin-engine seaplane carrying camera equipment and supplies for the shoot crashed into the set, killing eleven cast and crewmembers. That was the end of that shoot, as you might have already surmised.

The lump in my throat was insurmountable. My heart raced. Could this really be happening in my time? Why was I the one to witness this madness?

Before I could even research whether or not there was ever a horror film shoot on a Fall Equinox, I received a message. As if on cue.

It was from modranicht76.

They were back. The message was simple.

No. Not yet.

It was too much. Someone or something pretending to be an ally, a friend, was manipulating me.

Goading me into uncovering the full extent of what lay just underneath the surface. That whole iceberg theory. It was all right there. A massive, festering iceberg made of evil and sinister intent just waiting to be stumbled upon by the fake brave and the stupid tough. I feel like I've been—

Wait. Do you hear that? You *must* this time. It was unmistakable. Is it just me? Something is in my living room again. Just wait right here. Don't go anywhere.

* * *

Are you sure you didn't hear anything? I swear the noise traced back to here just like last time. Someone is messing with me. With *us*. You're just as much a part of this as I am now. What's that? Oh no, there's no getting out of it anymore. You've already heard too much. Might as well see it to the end. At least we're not alone in this, right? Curiosity loves company. That's the saying, correct? I think it is. Yes, it most definitely is.

Copasetic? Excellent. Where was I? Right. Fall Equinox. It must be happening soon. There's no other way around it. It's coming for us all and we have to stop it. Yes. We. I need your help in this. We can make sure the fourth door never opens. Whatever it is, it cannot be a good thing for this world.

We have to find Ford. Or Simon. Or both. modranicht76. They must hold the key. Maybe they are Ford. Or Simon. Or they are all one. It all makes sense now!

Before I forget, I'm reminded of a rare interview with Brynner in his later years. It was after he was diagnosed with lung cancer but before it rendered him at a disadvantage to speak. A journalist for a local affiliate newsmagazine show asked him if he had any stories about unfinished or stalled projects in his career.

It remains unknown whether or not the interviewer knew about *The Demon of Noel Crossing* or was just fishing for an interesting or fun answer to a seemingly innocent question. Regardless of the intent, Brynner's reaction to the question is the most interesting part of the video. For the briefest of seconds, Brynner's eyes darted to a corner of the room never shown. If you're not fully paying attention to the clip, you'd absolutely miss it. It's so fleeting and that's what makes it so alarming. Who was he looking at? *What* was he looking at? Did something follow him all those years after the disaster in Bumpass, lurking in the shadows, watching his every move? Did something follow the others as well?

Yul Brynner died of lung cancer in 1985. William Holden died after falling and hitting his head on a table while he was heavily intoxicated. The year was 1981. Fay Wray died peacefully in her sleep in 2004.

What's the connection? A good number of sources insist that Wray knew what was transpiring. Brynner and Holden were less receptive to the ceremony. Thus, the shadows followed them for the rest of their lives until they died under less-than-peaceful circumstances.

Tasteless? Where's the proof, you say? I sympathize with you and your line of logic.

During one of Holden's drunken benders near the end of his life, more than one acquaintance recalls him ranting about a film that no one could ever place happening. A movie in South America. People killed. Some*thing* that wouldn't leave him be despite him staying quiet for a decade. It just added to the urban legend of D.R. Ford and the four doorways to the abyss.

Until Brynner's death, many claimed he had strange episodes of seeing someone that wasn't there in the room with him. If only for mere seconds, but seconds nonetheless.

What did Holden and Brynner do that Wray refrained from? Why was she given a long life and they suffered painful deaths? Who would be next? Which star of stage and screen might be the key to the fourth doorway and the catalyst for another massacre?

You would think that in light of all this, I would find the nearest rock to hide under. Get gone. Disappear. You would think that. But I feel closer to the truth than any time since I started this journey. This quest for answers. I know that the documentary must happen. Only I can make it manifest. Spread the truth to the whole world. Only then can we prevent the fourth doorway from opening. The Fall Equinox must be kept sacred.

The cinematographer of *The Demon of Noel Crossing*, Lucio Gonzetti, has agreed to be my cameraman. It took a lot of convincing, but he now sees it my way. He knows the truth is the quickest way to ending all of this.

Even though the film's makeup artist Maria Fancher killed herself less than a year after the church fire, she took time out of her busy schedule to call me personally a few days ago and let me know I had her full support. I can't wait to interview her tomorrow. She sounds anxious to tell me everything.

Gonzetti and I are traveling to Bumpass this weekend to document the ruins of the set of *The Demon of Noel Crossing*. The Winter Solstice is nigh and it will be the perfect time to capture the location in all of its ghostlike glory. It's going to be so surreal to see it in the flesh. Feel it. What transpired there more than forty years ago. Some of my sources said they will meet us there under cover of night. You're coming too, right? You've come this far, after all. I won't hear anything to the contrary. Your attendance will make our crew a strong fourteen.

On top of that amazing turn of events, modranicht76 has informed me they plan on fully funding the documentary shoot to the end. Talk about serendipity. It's all coming together. The truth will out all of this evil and suffering. I'm so glad you've agreed to join me on this adventure. There's no turning back even if you wanted to.

Shog-Na'Goth demands it all be known. The Equinox will be kept sacred.

For *them*.

GOD REST YE SCARY SANTAMEN

I wasn't exactly sure why, but at the very moment I embedded my ax into the bloated stomach of that obsequious, uncanny Kris Kringle lookalike, I felt compelled to finally confess to Derek my Santa Claus fetish.

Wait. I feel like I might have started a tad too late. Let me rewind a bit.

* * *

Derek and I had been planning our big hideaway vacation to Dover Beach in Maine for what felt like years. It was probably only eight months, but still. Perception is reality.

December in Dover Beach meant that the town changed its name to Jingle Beach and hosted its annual March of Santas Lookalike Contest and Parade. They started doing it in the mid-80s as a gimmick to boost tourism and the thing stuck. People from all over the world came to celebrate the holidays and swelled the town's population to more than triple. At least for a few weeks. Santa cosplay enthusiasts from around the globe and every walk of life waited all year to descend upon the sleepy surfside hamlet and show off their yuletide stuff. Even Guy Fieri did an episode there once dressed as Santa. Not that that was a draw in any way for us.

I'd been with Derek for a few years now and I was dying to share with him my love for all things Christmas by way of a picturesque, small-town escape filled with sleigh rides, spiked lattes, tacky sweaters, and lots of alone time. Our first year together he was away on business and our second year as a couple saw me catch food poisoning from PF Chang's. Don't ask. Okay, it was the Bang Bang Shrimp. Does me in every time.

This year, there was nothing standing in our way. Both our families balked when we said we were going by ourselves this year. They thought we were eloping. After we talked them off that ledge, we reassured them that next year they would have us all to themselves. That's what we told them, anyways.

I always thought of Derek as a taller, slimmer, handsomer, better-looking version of me. I called him my little aspiration. He claimed he thought it was funny, but he never actually laughed when I addressed him as such. Another reason I loved him so. The wherewithal to roll with my corny-ass punches.

About the Santa fetish. I told you I was going to get back to that. For what seemed like forever, I've had a huge crush on the jolly old fat man. Which is weird, because I've never been into bears, per se. Come to think of it, I've never really had a preference. Except for Derek. He's one hell of a preference. Anyway, I think I can trace it all back to high school when my tenth-grade obsession, Matt Dinsmore, played Santa Claus at our holiday talent show. The whole thing was an ungodly dumpster fire but when Matt came on stage and did his rendition of "Santa Baby" *as* Santa, it turned my whole world upside down. I was marked as a Kringle-fied chubby chaser for life.

Of course, I was terrified of telling Derek about it. What would he say? There was nothing more I wanted than to get him into a Santa suit and deck the goddamn halls, but I couldn't risk losing him over something so random. And weird. But hot. Really hot.

I pictured Jingle Beach like one of those towns straight out of a Hollywood movie. Clean, overly festive, bucolic locals galore, and lots of baked goods. Like way too much. Do they bake that stuff just for the movie or do they just go to the store and buy it? How much is too much? I had to find out.

Our drive up there was uneventful yet deceptively pleasant. I tried to program the Christmas music like a celebrity DJ at Club Noel but Derek had reached his limit of holiday tunes about halfway through our eight-hour trip. I couldn't blame him. Even I felt like I was forcing the issue. Oh well. It was nice while it lasted.

When there was a lull in his Spotify playlist of 80s new wave B-sides, he asked me "Do you really love Christmas this much?"

"I mean, yeah I love it. What's not to love?"

"Yeah, but *this* much?"

I understood what he meant immediately.

"Look, it's just a different kind of vacation. Something I've wanted to do for a while. After this week, we can mothball the whole North Pole mood and find some other adventure. I'm just happy we can get away together for a change. Just us. That's all."

It worked. Derek shifted into easygoing mode just as the next song was amping up. He reached for my hand and it was the only thing I wanted in that moment.

"Sounds good. How about the running of the bulls?" Derek said with a smirk as he glanced at me.

"Uh, let's find something in between those two extremes first. Jesus."

We both laughed it all off and I could tell he was really looking forward to this time away just as much as I was. Maybe even more. Maybe this could be it. I could finally tell him my secret desire. I was so excited at the possibility that I almost blurted it out right then and there.

Patience, Owen. Patience.

We reached the former Dover Beach with stomachs full of hot chocolate and lobster rolls. A seaside eatery on the way up had really hit the spot. I almost told him about my Santa predilections there, but I choked a bit on my lobster roll and Derek had to step in and kind of save my life. You can't really blurt out a secret fetish after a near-death experience. Not when you have lobster breath.

Main street was just how it looked in the photos on the website. They had a huge banner hanging from two vintage lamp posts on opposite sides of the street. Emblazoned on it was "WELCOME TO JINGLE BEACH – HOME OF THE MARCH OF SANTAS!" I loved it. It was comforting and tacky all at once.

People scurried here and there up and down and across the street as we rolled down Main at a snail's pace. Derek's eagle eyes scanned for our hotel.

"It should be just up ahead." He mumbled as he kept his eyes peeled on the advancing facades.

"There it is." I saw it first and stuck my tongue out at Derek with a playful chuckle. He smiled back and prepared to turn in towards our accommodations.

The Surfside Inn. One of a handful of hotels on the main drag we could have stayed. It had the most Christmas-y potential based on the photos I perused online. The only thing, though, was that it didn't have a single Christmas decoration on it. None to be found. Like it was any other day of the year.

"Not too shabby." Derek admitted. Of course he'd love the one sans holiday cheer.

"Same goes for you." I kissed him on the cheek, ready for this vacation to start in earnest. As he parked, I was already hopping out to go check in.

And then I saw the weirdest thing as I hurried into the hotel. A guy, clearly a Santa lookalike based on his white beard and approximate age, shuffled aimlessly down the sidewalk toward me. Empty eyes, mumbling something low and strange.

Thing was, though, he was skinny as could be. No bowl full of jelly to be found. Looked like a mummified member of ZZ Top. As I grabbed the door to go inside, his eyes met mine and the stare he gave me raised my hackles more than a little. Maybe he was upset at himself for not being method enough to gain some legit Santa poundage. Truth was, I didn't really want to know. Those eyes. No thanks.

*　*　*

Inside the hotel was as normal and undecorated as the outside. I made a beeline for the front desk and caught the concierge just as he was getting off the phone. A tall, bespectacled man with a weird horseshoe mustache that jangled all over his face when he sniffed.

"How do you not sneeze all the time with that magnificent face piece?" I thought I'd lighten the mood a little even though I realized the mood hadn't even been defined yet. Vintage me.

The concierge, Marcello if you believed his gold name tag, huffed up and bristled a bit. I could tell right away there'd be no witty banter to be had here. Oh well.

"Whatever do you mean, my good sir?"

Well, at least he was polite in his humorlessness. A plus. I guess?

"Checking in, please. Schmidt."

I hated my last name. It was so blunt. Schmidt. I mean, I had no complaints familywise. Except for that name. It never settled with me. Now Derek, on the other hand, had a winner of a last name. Von Bargen. Derek Von Bargen. Owen Von Bargen. I almost reserved the room under Von Bargen. I was close.

"Will you be taking in the sights during your stay, my good sir?"

Huh?

"Are there...people who don't take in the sights...when they're on vacation here?"

"Everyone has a story, I'm sure, my good sir."

"O...kay. Sounds good. And yes, we will be taking in the sights. Any recommends?"

"If you find yourself out late at night, please do refrain from following any sounds of sleigh bells."

Was that a recommendation? What in the blue hell was happening right now?

"Uh… Wise advice, my good sir, wise advice indeed."

I harrumphed on top of that to a parodic level. I'm not sure if he fully appreciated it.

"We can have a bellboy take your bags to your room. Please have a pleasant stay here in the enchanted confines of Jingle Beach, my—"

"My good sir!" I bellowed with more than a little mock zest.

And with that, I had had enough of the routine. I headed back outside to help Derek with our bags when that same guy, that emaciated Santa wannabe, was stopped dead in front of the doors. Blocking my escape from this odd waystation in between Christmas and a random Tuesday in February.

"You're safe in here. No Christmas cheer."

The way the guy said it was both hopeful and terrified. I couldn't decide which one I preferred more. Instead, I just made for the door with a polite brush of my hand on his shoulder. It felt icy cold like a fresh snowdrift. And he smelled like someone had dumped a giant box of gingerbread mix on top of him. Not an unpleasant smell under normal circumstances, but this was not that.

"You should probably bundle up. Layers help with the cold, you know. Excuse me."

"Safe! Safe inside where there's no cheer!"

This guy was annoying me and rattling my nerves in equal measures. As I made it past him and pushed open the front door, I could hear an employee trying to usher him outside and away from their establishment. I hurried extra quick so that guy and his eyes weren't directly on me as he left right behind me.

I made it to our car and I think I scared Derek a bit with my abrupt return. He jumped in his seat and patted his chest gently. Rolled down his window.

"Jesus. You scared some pee out of me, I think. We good?"

I looked back to see where Diet Santa was. Nowhere to be seen. Not even shuffling down the sidewalk in the distance somewhere. Just gone. I turned back to Derek and just nodded.

* * *

After settling into our room and freshening up, we were determined to paint the town red. And green. Well, I was. Derek was a good sport and went along for the ride. I could tell he was tired and just wanted to nap, but I wanted to see all this legendary Jingle Beach cheer in the daylight. For posterity.

Our tacky sweater game was in full effect. Mine was a plum turtleneck with two reindeers nuzzling the crap out of each other surrounded by cheering elves. It was elaborate and sweet. Two of my favorite adjectives. Derek's was a bit more traditional. A fluffy sky-blue V-neck with Santa and Mrs. Claus joyriding in a sleigh in the middle of a winter wonderland. I picked that one out for him. It accentuated his near-perfectly chiseled physique. Two great tastes that taste great together.

As we walked through the most decorated street I've ever been on, I kinda sorta marveled at how intricately the place was decked out. Animatronic nutcrackers and elves greeted people walking into various shops, a miniature train chugging around a massive track suspended in the air just above the streetlamps. It seemed to go on forever. The train whistle reminded me of trips to my grandmother's house for Christmas. She would blow her own little train whistle whenever cookies were fresh out of the oven for us kids to devour.

They even had a giant glass snowman filled with jellybeans. It must have been about twelve feet tall. You could guess how many jellybeans were in there and win what? All those jellybeans? It sounded like a pain in the butt of a prize. But still, very festive.

I was really getting into the seasonal mood, but I sensed Derek was still on autopilot, taking in sights but refusing to let them affect him in any way. So, I tried the direct approach.

"Thank you for being here with me for this. It's beautiful and so are you."

Okay, so that might have been a little on the nose. But I was being honest. Sometimes that's what needs to be said.

Derek just smiled and squeezed his arm around me even tighter. I'd take whatever I could get at that point.

Derek wanted a coffee and I wanted baked goods. We split the difference and found a quaint cafe called Baker's Dozen that specialized in both. I ended up getting an apple turnover with cinnamon whipped cream. Just criminally delicious. And too big even for me to finish. Derek's spiked hot chocolate smelled pretty damn good from where I was sitting. I was never a huge fan of Bailey's in my sweet drinks per se, but I was willing to make an exception this time.

"Mind if I have a taste?"

You would have thought I'd just dug up the corpse of Derek's childhood dog the way he backed his whole body away from me whilst still seated in his chair.

"You can get your own, you know."

Wow. Okay, I wasn't going to let this morph into a public pissing match. I had to try another tack.

"Well, I can't finish this whole turnover myself. How about we share?"

"You never have a problem finishing too much food on your own. What's different today?"

Ouch. Sure, I wasn't exactly a Skinny Minnie, but I'm not a warthog, either.

"That's fine. I'll just bag this up and get my own drink. No worries."

Donnybrook averted. I knew he was just trying to start something as an excuse to go back to the room by himself. Not this time. I was in peak holiday mood and nothing could bring me down right now.

Except for Diet Santa staring at us through the window. From across the street.

"Hey. Hey, Derek. Do you see that guy?"

"Where?"

"Across the street. He's literally staring right at us."

After a moment, Derek spotted him. And then just said nothing. Just stared right back at him. To say it was unsettling was a gross understatement.

"What's with the staring contest?"

Derek was locked onto the guy and vice versa. I snapped my fingers in his face and oh boy, did he not like that.

"Get your fingers out of my face." My snap caused him to snap. I'd never seen him that angry before.

"What is going on with you, babe?"

"He told me we're going to be his soon."

Excuse me?

"What the hell are you talking about?"

I looked out to where the guy was just seconds ago. Gone again. I was starting to get a truly uneasy feeling. All the spiked hot chocolate in the world probably wouldn't make it go away, I feared.

* * *

Walking back to the hotel was more than a little awkward. The near fight, the scraggly Santa. All of it seemed dead set on ruining this trip. But I wasn't giving up.

"How about we rest up and later we can go for a walk on the beach. I hear it's the perfect kickstart for some romance."

I thought Derek was going to respond with something snide again, but after a pregnant pause, he smiled and simply said "Sure. I'd like that."

Trip saved. I was determined to make this work for me. For us. A little Christmas cheer can go a long way. Especially if there's beach sex involved.

* * *

Back at the hotel, I tried in vain to put the moves on Derek. All he was interested in was a big fat nap. He was still down for the beach later, though. I called it a wash and decided to get some answers about the nagging feelings tugging at my subconscious. They were getting stronger now that my surroundings were quiet.

I made my way back down to the lobby where I failed to spot a single soul. It couldn't have been later than four in the afternoon and there wasn't a single person to be found. Except for Marcello. My old friend.

I tried to make eye contact with him as I approached the front desk, I even shuffled my shoes loudly on the carpet. Something to get him to look up. Nothing. Was he actively ignoring me?

"Ahem." I actually said the word "ahem" instead of clearing my throat. Very Arch Karen of me, I will admit.

Marcello responded without meeting my gaze, like he was expecting me all along.

"Mr. Schmidt, how can I help you this time?"

This time? Was I that much of a pain in the ass? I could only remember speaking to this guy one other time. When we checked in. Hours ago.

"Got somewhere to be, my good sir?" I wasn't going to give up on making this stiff laugh. Hell, I'd settle for a muffled snicker at this point.

"I'm terribly busy at the moment, so if there's something I can assist you with, I would be delighted to do so immediately."

There was that polite rudeness again.

"What's with the lack of decorations for this hotel? Is the owner a Jehovah's Witness?"

"It's to ward off the blood curse that haunts this town. You chose the best hotel for your stay."

I heard what he said just fine but my brain demanded a refund.

"Pardon? Blood…blood curse…?"

"Absolutely, my good sir. Started in 1983 with a pagan ritual performed on the beach. Turned many townsfolk and tourists into demons. Ran amok. It was a whole thing. Quite the nasty aftermath."

This guy must have thought I was a real up-your-nose-with-a-rubber-hose asshole. I preferred the snide, condescending banter to this shit. I wanted to tell him to eff off and just head back to the room, but I had one more question and I was damned if I wasn't going to ask it.

"What's with the dollar store Santa roaming around town?"

"This town is host to a Santa lookalike parade and contest. You will have to be a bit more specific, my good sir."

"The skinny creep scaring the crap out of people and flexing his telepathy skills."

"Ah yes, him. He is some sort of alchemist, I believe. A sorcerer, too."

"A what?"

"That is how he introduced himself, if I remember him correctly."

Huh.

"Well, thanks for the chat. You've got a fantastic imagination and I salute you."

I wanted Derek. I wanted a walk on the beach. I wanted away from this wacko loon.

"I would advise remaining in your room when the late hour arrives. Once you hear sleigh bells on the beach, it is already too late. Much safer indoors. Much safer in here, my good sir."

"I'll take that advisement under advisement. Thanks. My good sir."

I tried to keep myself from rolling my eyes until I had turned away from him, but I had already started as soon as I finished speaking. I caught his mustache bristle a bit before my head was all the way round and facing the elevator.

Alchemist? Sleigh bells? Was this the roleplaying adventure nerd hotel or something? Did I pay extra for that? What the hell was going on? I knew Derek would be even less enthusiastic about this nonsense. I decided not to even mention I talked to Marstachio back there.

It was time for a romantic stroll on the beach. Come hell or high water.

* * *

So, I may have oversold the beach a tad. Turns out, sea breezes in December were like low key Arctic winds. Even with our heavy sweaters and coats, it was a struggle to stroll with comfort and dignity. Even the thought of beach sex out here in this weather made my pelvis pucker.

It was beautiful, though. The moon was high and combined with the sand to create an otherworldly glow up and down the shoreline. Derek had his neutral face on, and it was really starting to annoy me. Sure, it was kind of inhospitable out here, but it was romantic, for Pete's sake. The rhythmic lapping of the tide said so.

We were basically dragging each other by the arm to keep moving forward so we could say we went for a walk on the beach when neither one of us had any desire to actually put the work in. After a day full of sneering and sniping and snapping, Derek was about to incur my full wrath. I was ready to unload on him now that we didn't have a captive audience.

"So, is this the part where you tell me what your deal is? Or do I have to hire a private investigator to find exactly where the bug that crawled up your ass is located?"

The look on Derek's face signified he knew this was coming. His opening salvo was surprisingly calm.

"You know I don't like Christmas. I'm doing my best."

"Yeah. But why? Why act like a jerk all day like it wasn't your choice to come here?"

"Well, it wasn't. You made sure of that."

"How the hell did you not have a choice? Are you an adult or not?"

Derek stopped. He still hadn't raised his voice or rolled his eyes yet. A minor miracle for the day.

"You know what? Fine. Here you go. When I was fifteen, I was attacked by a mall Santa. I worked at the Orange Julius in the mall and after my shift, in the parking lot, the fucking shopping mall Santa Claus tackled me, beat the shit out of me and threw me in his car. He took me to his apartment and proceeded to drunkenly serenade me with all the Christmas carols he could half-remember in his blottoed state. Oh, and to top it all off, he puked his mall food court Chinese dinner all over me right before the cops showed up."

"How did you know it was Chinese food?"

"I'm out." Derek started back toward the hotel. My humor reflex had struck at the wrong time.

"Jesus, Derek. Why didn't you tell me this before? That's a pretty big detail to leave out before coming on a Christmas vacation to a Christmas town drenched in Christmas cheer!"

"I just wanted you to be happy. I know this trip means a lot to you. I thought I could do it. I really, really thought I could. But today was a struggle. I don't think I can do another day here."

Before I could respond to him, I could have sworn I heard sleigh bells further down the beach.

"Do you hear that?"

"What?! Did you hear what I just said?"

"Sleigh bells…"

I have no idea why I followed the sound. Even after Marcello the Mustache Man warned me not to. Maybe it was my sense of adventure. Maybe it was my idiotic way of trying to keep our vacation going as it was crumbling down around me.

Or maybe I was just trying to avoid processing what Derek just confessed to me. It meant my secret fantasy was probably going to remain a secret.

"Where are you going? Owen!"

His voice trailed off as I jogged toward the sound. As soon as I cleared a small dune, I could see a green bonfire up ahead. A holiday bonfire? Weird for sure, but I couldn't see any sign of sleigh bells even though they were still filling my ears.

As I got closer to the fire, I could see a figure. A man. And that's when it all fell into place and I realized I was the biggest fool in Fooltown. The mayor of Fooltown for life. There, throwing what looked like sand into the growing emerald bonfire, was him. The skinny, homeless, Santa wannabe creep. I could hear Derek calling after me, his voice getting closer and closer. All I could focus on, though, was that man and his creaky, nasally chanting. I couldn't make out exactly what he was saying, but it didn't sound pleasant. Guttural, angry. Germanic? Something inhospitable, for sure.

"Owen, for God's sake—" Derek had caught up to me and instead of finishing his sentence, he saw what I was fixed on and pulled on my arm.

"Let's go. Now."

I wanted to go. I really did. But as soon as Derek spoke, the scraggly Santa wannabe locked eyes on us and smiled. It was the first time I saw his teeth. They were all pointed. He pushed his tongue out through his razor-sharp teeth and it made a wet, squishy sound that made me gag.

"Hello, big boys! You're just in time!"

As he was rubbing his hands together in excitement, another couple approached from the other direction. Probably from a hotel with a shitload of decorations. Yet we were both in the same predicament. They were a cute, chubby couple with matching tacky Grinch sweaters. As if there were such a thing as a non-tacky Grinch sweater.

"Oh. Sorry to interrupt your—" The guy of the couple said, not really sure what they were interrupting. His girl was already backing away before he even began speaking.

"Oh, not so fast. This is perfect! Four for the price of two!" Diet Santa squealed.

And with that, he reached into the green flame of the bonfire and scooped some out like he was scooping up a snowball. Then, he threw the fireball at the couple and shouted something that sounded like *"Gin and tonic!"* but in reality it was more like *"Gine ton!"* even though I had no idea what that language even was.

As the fireball hit the stunned couple, they fell to the ground and writhed in what looked like agony. I wasn't sure.

"We. Have. To. Go. Now." Derek was trying to sound like the strong one, like he always did, but I could tell he was scared shitless.

I turned to run, but as I did, the couple started to change. Not like anything I would ever expect them to change into. At all. Their bellies expanded to a much larger size, ripping their clothes in the process. Their hair turned stark white and grew down to their shoulders. They both grew silver beards that reached their sternums. I could hear them making some kind of noise, but what I initially thought was howling or moaning was something else entirely.

"HO HO HO HO HO…"

They were bellowing like Santa Claus. Jolly and guttural. Deep, supernatural belly laughs. It was the most terrifying thing I had ever heard in my entire life.

Derek pulled on my arm hard and I needed no other prompt at that point. We both turned and ran as fast as we could through the high sand. Diet Santa's voice rang out behind us.

"Get them, my pets!"

The sound of ho-ho-ho-ing picked up and followed us the whole way as we sprinted across the beach and back to Main Street. We weren't even thinking about where our hotel was. We just wanted off that beach. I didn't have to ask Derek to know he was thinking the exact same thing.

As we reached the main drag and the sand had disappeared for good, I noticed the Santa belly laughing had also vanished. Were we safe? Was it only a beach thing? Limited range of control for Homeless Santa? I leaned against the local hardware store and attempted to catch my breath. Derek was further out in the street. It looked like a ghost town. The place shut down earlier than any place I had ever been before. Almost right at sundown.

"Owen. Let's go. We should—"

Before he could finish, I felt a tight, strong hand close in on my throat. Followed immediately by the sensation of being lifted up several feet off the ground. And then, I was flying. For a few seconds, it felt nice, then my body met the plate glass window of the hardware store. As I hit the ground, I could hear Derek shouting my name, followed by the sounds of a scuffle. That's the last thing I remember before the lights went out.

* * *

I had no idea how long I had actually been out for. Seconds? Minutes? I knew it wasn't hours because I could hear Derek grunting and breathing hard just outside. He was still fighting off something out there.

I can't remember if I stood up first or reached for the ax that lay next to me in the mess of shattered glass and destroyed displays, but before I knew it, I was up and armed without even surveying the extent of my injuries.

Right away, I saw Derek fending off both of the…santamen…weresantas? Why didn't the woman turn into a Mrs. Claus thing? Was that sexist?

They were gnashing their teeth, trying to bite Derek. He was keeping them at bay with forearms and elbows to their bodies and faces. Derek was the very definition of a big strong man and he was showing it right there and then. As well as he was doing, I knew he needed my help.

I jumped through the now windowless hole in the hardware store and charged at one of them. I wasn't sure which one was the guy or girl anymore. Like it even mattered. I swung my ax at the nearest one to me and planted it in its back. It definitely yowled in pain, but it didn't drop to the ground or die or anything. It just kept attacking my Derek.

"Hit it again!" I could tell Derek was getting tired and his voice was full of fear. I had to end this.

I yanked my ax out of the santaman's back and caused it to spin around to face me. Teeth out and gnashing. Its arms outstretched toward me now. In a moment of sheer panic and pure reflex, I struck out at the weresanta and hit it squarely in the stomach. My blade punctured it quick and clean, like it was meant to go there.

The howl that emanated from the Santa thing was sorrowful and accepting all at once. The other weresanta that was still attacking Derek stopped and howled in pain at the sound of its partner's death throes.

As my axed santaman dropped to the ground, I tried to yank the ax head out of its stomach but it was a mighty struggle. I had to embed my foot into the bulbous tummy and pull mightily on the ax for it to finally come out, tearing the santaman's midsection from groin to sternum. Hot, steaming green jelly avalanched out and onto the street. The sheer volume of the stench made me puke immediately.

I wiped away the vomit on my mouth with my sleeve and I wanted to stammer *what the eff* but Derek beat me to it.

"What the fuck?!" He seemed more surprised than I was, which felt impossible given the circumstances.

"Heads up!" I tossed my ax to Derek; confident he'd know what to do with it. As he caught it, his attacking santaman grabbed his arm and took a chunk out of it with its chomping pearly whites. Derek yelped in shock and pain but managed to bury the ax in the weresanta's stomach with one swift, quick thrust.

And so, another pile of steamy green jelly was on the pavement and another transformed jolly old fat man lay dead. Derek dropped to the ground, holding his bitten arm tight to his chest.

"How'd I do?" He was starting to lose consciousness and drooped over to one side, almost laying down on the pavement completely.

I knew what was coming next without having to see it. Before it could even begin to happen, I grabbed Derek and dragged him to the alley adjacent to the hardware store. I propped him up against the brick wall belonging to said store and checked his wound. It looked like a deep bite from an average human set of teeth. There was blood but nowhere near as much as there would have been had it been some sort of wild animal.

Or a werewolf, Owen. Or a werewolf.

The level of surreal insanity I had found myself in was so extreme that my brain just shut it out completely and focused only on what I could actually, physically do.

I ripped off a section of my sweater sleeve. The one not covered in my own puke. I wrapped it tight around his bite and tied it off with all the strength I had left.

I looked into Derek's eyes and figured I had to say something profound. If not now, when? "I guess this would be a bad time to tell you I have a Santa Claus fetish."

Not exactly my finest moment, but it was on my mind. I expected Derek to dress me down even in his current state; instead he just laughed, ignoring the pain. His smile destroyed me inside.

"You're bleeding."

I thought it was me talking to Derek. But it was him talking to me.

"A lot."

I checked myself out and sure enough, I was bleeding all over from the glass window I had sailed through moments ago. The adrenaline had masked the pain and any awareness that anything was even wrong with me. Now that I was coming down from it all, I could feel slices in my skin all over my body.

"I'm fine. We need to get you to a hospital. Who knows if they had rabies or something."

"Rabies?" Derek coughed and laughed at the same time. A trickle of white liquid dribbled from the corner of his mouth when he coughed. It smelled like…

…*Milk?*

"Owen…you saw what happened. Saw what they became. Do I have to say it…out loud?"

"Weresantas. There. I said it. Look, Derek, I'm sorry. Sorry for all of it. We should never have come here. I'd rather spend Christmas at your parents for the next thirty God damn years. Let's get out of here."

Derek smiled and nodded. "It's okay. I feel pretty good. I—" He coughed up what looked like half-digested milk and cookies. His breath stank of peppermint and cinnamon. And milk. I was immediately off desserts at that point.

"Merry Christmas, Owen."

He tried to kiss me one last time, but the transformation had taken hold. His stomach bulged out, busting his pants and sweater. His hair turned shaggy and silver and a big, bushy white beard started to grow on his clean-shaven face. I had never seen him with facial hair before. It was startling even out of context.

I knew what I had to do. I leaned in and kissed him softly. My ax dug into his expanding stomach quietly. It was quick and easy as his stomach enlarged right onto the blade, popping it like a fleshy balloon. He died in the last throes of his transformation.

My sobbing sounded like someone else's. Someone who had been through a lifetime of tragedy and it was finally all coming out at once. That wasn't me. It couldn't be me.

"Don't cry, my friend. Your luck is about to change."

I knew that voice right away. It set the hairs on my skin aflame. I turned from Derek to see the scraggly, skinny wannabe Santa standing in the alleyway. All around him were dozens and dozens of newly transformed weresantas. Locals and tourists ho-ho-hoing in their torn, ragged clothes with their distended bellies jiggling in the night air. Their white hair and beards glistened like shark teeth in the late hour. It seemed my moment had arrived. Certain death or the remainder of my life as a skinwalking Pere Noel.

"Come over here and take your bite like a man."

I stood up. Feeling defiant, I raised my ax, ready to strike. Just a dozen or so feet away from Diet Santa and his army of Kris Kringles.

"And what do you think that will do?"

I stared at my ax. So far it was two for two. I liked my odds.

"Let me guess. 1984. Blood curse. Pagan bullshit. Am I close?"

Diet Santa laughed. "Oh, indeed. But it seems I overestimated the amount of Christmas cheer in this godforsaken town. Too much of it. Much too much of it. Instead of raising an army of yule demons, it seems I have created something else entirely.

"Just say it. Santamen. Weresantas."

"You just said it for me. It's not exactly what I had been planning, but I suppose beggars can't be choosers. Especially around Christmas."

At this point, I was out of things to say. Just the thought of being chomped to death by an army of weresantas took up all the real estate in my brain. As it should, right?

Then, he did something even a corpse would have thought was a bad idea.

He raised his arms to the sky and bellowed "Hail Krampus! Hail Belsnickel! Hail Satan!"

Hmmm.

The throng of weresantas surrounding him, upon hearing those words, collectively gasped and proceeded to pounce on Elderly Waif Santa, gnashing teeth chewing on him posthaste. It was a disgusting sight. The old man was minced into mashed flesh faster than it took to blend a margarita.

It took me just a few seconds to realize that was my cue to make a quick exit. As the merry band of newly appointed gift givers finished snacking on their would-be master, I quietly fast-walked back to the Surfside Inn. I was fully expecting to be body checked or bitten by an errant santaman, but eerily enough, all was uneventful. I made my way inside and rushed to the elevator, hoping to barricade myself in my room to wait for dawn.

* * *

Marcello was still at the front desk. Did this guy ever go home? I guess it was probably wise on his part that he didn't. He took one look at my bloody, frazzled frame and sniffed. That mustache blustering all over his face as he did.

"You'll be safe in here, good sir."

"No shit, Marcello. No fucking shit."

I didn't wait for a reply. Whatever he said wouldn't have mattered anyway. Derek was gone. I needed to get to my room and stay there. Even if it was safe in the lobby, as Mr. Mustache insisted.

* * *

Dawn came and with it, no weresanta attacks. I had stayed planted firmly in the middle of my king-sized bed, knees in my chest and arms wrapped tight around myself.

Had I done the right thing? Did I really have to kill Derek? Maybe we could have lived like that. Me and my Santa Derek. We could have just told everyone we were all in on the Santa mood and Derek wanted to look like more of a manly man. An elderly, overweight Norwegian lumberjack. Something like that. What if he had bitten one of our family members? *All* of our family members? How would I prevent that? Should I have tried? Did I really love Derek? I just killed him. It didn't take me long to even decide.

I forced my brain to shut its mouth and I got cleaned up, packed, and checked out without another word to Marcello. He knew. He didn't have to say anything and neither did I. Sleigh bells late at night. The beach. The whole deal. I just wanted to go home.

As I pulled out of the Surfside Inn, I didn't see anything outwardly sinister in the streets and alleyways. But I looked closer. And when I looked closer, when I really tried to look for something, I could see people. People staggering in and out of view. Their tattered clothes and their big pot bellies. Men and women. No beards or white hair.

But I knew. I knew exactly what they were. What they would become again at night when the sleigh bells rang out in the distance.

I had the feeling that the town would clean up after itself. How else could they keep getting away with…whatever they were getting away with? Derek was gone, and it would probably stay that way. The curse of Jingle Beach was alive and well. Maybe just not in the way it originally occurred.

I had no interest in sticking around for the Santa Lookalike contest. It had pretty much already happened for me up close and personal.

I sped up, trying to get the image of those staggering people with their fat bellies and torn clothes out my head. I turned off Main Street and headed for the highway. For home.

The smell of cinnamon and gingerbread was still with me, though. I had a feeling it would never go away.

Needless to say, I no longer have a Santa fetish.

P.W.B. (PLEASE WRITE BACK)

TINSEL TRAUMA

October 10

Dear Santa,

My name is Emily Adams and I'm nine years old. Almost ten, actually. My mom said you're super real still and I shood write you myself to ask for what I want. No drawing any pictures. No magazine cut outs. Just my words and that's it she said. I told her she was being too strick on me but now that I'm writing this letter, I'm pretty sure she's just trying to get me to be a better writer or sumthing like that.

Anyway before I forget I want to make sure I ask for a vintige poleroid camera with plenty of film and a vintige sholder strap to go with it. Something cool like old lether or crush velvet. Can you make that happen, Mr. Claus? I think I've been pretty good. I made a few faces at my mom now and then when she tells me to do something like clean my room and I fight with my little brother Gavin every now and then but other then that not much else to put me on the notty list. At leased I'm onest, right?

I hope you're real for real. I didn't want too believe this year but my mom convinced me pretty much. She's like that with a lot of things. I had my dowts last year when I didn't get what I asked for. Do you remember what I reely asked for last year? If you do, you got a believer for the rest of my life and yours. That's a long time I think.

83

Sinseerly,

Emily A.

P.S.: PWB

(that means Please Write Back)

24th of October

Dear Emily,

Happy Halloween, almost! By the time I hear from you again and I reply to that letter the big Pumpkin Day will be over again for another year. Don't tell Mrs. Claus but Halloween is my favorite holiday! I know, you're probably wondering why it's not Christmas. That one's a close second. Ha! What about you? Do you like Halloween? Are you dressing up as anyone or anything? Please let me know!

As for your request, I think I can make that happen. Vintage Polaroid cameras are a passion of mine as well! We have that in common, at least. I think the occasional rude face and the odd fight with your brother is perfectly normal. You have a good heart and love your family dearly and that counts more than anything else as far as I'm concerned. And as far as *my list* is concerned! Ha!

You just keep listening to your mom and doing the best you can in school and I'll take care of the rest. Deal? I think I'm going to dress up as the Stay-Puft marshmallow man for Halloween. Have you ever seen *Ghostbusters*? It's one of my favorite movies!

Well, I'll say goodbye for now and I eagerly await your next letter. Thank you for trying your best to believe in me. Every little bit helps keep this Christmas boat afloat!

Sinseerly (I like that!),

Your friend,

Mr. C

P.S.: It was an accordion. You asked for a vintage polka accordion from Germany or Austria. Sorry! I tried but someone else beat you to the punch on that one. Only so many vintage polka accordions from either Germany or Austria to go around that aren't currently being used. I hope the new bike suited you well. I know it's not too original of a gift, but I work with what I have. You're not too mad at me, are you?

P.P.S.: PWB

(that means Please Write Back!)

November 7

Dear Santa,

I was a zombie princess for Halloween. Like I had a Cinderella dress and crown and shoes all worn and ripped up and everything. My dad put a bunch of zombie makeup and fake blood all over me. It was pretty cool I gotta say. If you're gonna do something, mite as well do it right. That's what my mom says alot.

So how do you know about the accordion? I guess you're the real Santa then. Right? The only other thing would be that if my mom and dad are writing these letters to keep me believing in you. In Santa I mean.

Mom? Dad? Is this really you pretending to be Santa?

I wana believe but it's just so hard to these days. My grandma and grandpa are both dead. My uncle Kevin has canser. My dad says its something called stayge 4 or level 4 or something. It doesn't sound good. I used to go over to his house back when he wasn't sick and we'd watch old action movies from a long time ago when the good guys kicked people in the faces really hard. They were so much fun. I can't go over there any more. He's real sick and throws up a lot. I wish I could hug him but he looks like he wood snap into a bunch of pieces if I even touched him just a little bit.

I like *Ghostbusters*. It's one of Uncle Kevin's favorite movies. If you're really real, that's a weird fact about you. Miss Claus doesn't mind it when you go ghostbusting? Where do you trick or treat in the North Pole? I'm not sure I believe that like one hundred persent.

If you can make the poleroid thing happen, I would be pretty happy about it. I want to take some pictures of my uncle before it's to late. I hope he makes it to Christmas. Maybe you could send it a little early just in case?

PWB

Emily A.

TINSEL TRAUMA

21st of November

Dear Emily,

Do you remember when your grandma died and you wished in your bed one night to come to the North Pole to live with me and Mrs. Claus and all the elfs and my reindeer so you'd never ever be sad again? Well, I heard that wish. Maybe someday we can make that happen. We have plenty of room for executive toy designers and public relations representatives. Those are all just fancy words for Christmas super-secret agents! And you get paid for it too! In the meantime, you need to be closer to your parents and your Uncle Kevin. They need you so very much right now. Trust me.

I'll try to get you that Polaroid camera a little early maybe. Take all the pictures of your uncle you want. I'll provide plenty of film, too.

Do you remember which movies your Uncle Kevin let you watch? Was it Jean-Claude Van Damme or Chuck Norris? Or both? I love *Code of Silence* and *Kickboxer*. They're so much fun! Hi-yah! Ha!

My wife doesn't mind one bit that I go trick or treating as a Ghostbuster. Every now and then when she's feeling free-spirited she'll dress up as Gozer the Gozerian from the first Ghostbusters movie. You know, the lady who looks like she's covered in bubbles.

She kind of looks like Sheena Easton. She's a singer from the 80s. Ask your uncle about her! I really want my wife to try dressing up as Vigo the Carpathian one year soon. She's warming up to the idea, I think. That's the villain from *Ghostbusters II*. An underrated movie, Emily! That means it's not as bad as people once thought. That's a good word to remember. Underrated. You'll have to prove to a lot of people throughout your life that you're not underrated. That you're better than just underrated. That you're rated. I can tell you'll be something someday. Someone memorable.

Oh, and to answer your question, I trick or treat at all the elf houses and apartments. It's a lot of fun. There's also several Inuit communities up here that enjoy the holiday. They call me Goofy Gus whenever I come around. It's a term of endearment, I feel. Ha!

There's one thing I wanted to share with you about that. I think I can trust you to keep this between you and me. When I went trick or treating this year to the elfish suburbs just outside my warehouse outskirts, I witnessed something odd. Weird, even. It was funny, but a lot of the elfs were acting really strange. As if they were afraid of me but also scared of something else. They were jumpy. They didn't say much at all. Usually they're all a chatty bunch. It gave me the heebie jeebies, Emily. Do you know what those are? That's when something gives you the super creeps. I'm sure you've felt that before. Maybe late at night in bed when you think there's something in your closet or under your bed? That's how I felt about my friends staring creepily at me and mumbling something I couldn't understand.

The week following Halloween was also weird. They felt different. Cold. Distant. Not unfriendly, but definitely affected by something that seemed to frighten them greatly.

Anyhoo, I should probably end this letter now. It's getting pretty long and I don't want to bore you. I just hope we can be pen pals from now on. Things are getting weird up here and I could really use a friend. Sometimes at night I can feel something or someone watching me when Mrs. Claus is dead asleep, snoring like a sick walrus! Ha! Don't tell her I said that. And please don't show this letter to your parents. We don't want to get them involved. This is just between you and us. Okay?

Your friend,

Mr. C

PWB

December 5

Dear Santa,

My uncle Kevin dyed last week.

I mean, I know its not your fault, but the Polaroid camera came after the funeral. I put in here a picture of me in my dress from his funeral. My mom said I looked very respeckful in it. My favorite movie I watched with him was the one with the cop and the dog and they were a team fighting crime. I thought it was a pretty funny movie. Goofy and chessy but it made my uncle laugh. I miss hearing his laugh so much.

I'm sorry you had a weerd Halloween. Your friends sound like they're having a bad time all around. Maybe you should take them to the movies or by them some ice cream? That's what my dad or my uncle always did when I was feeling weird or sad. Made me feel better for sure.

Maybe they watched some movies that were way to scary? On second thought, maybe don't take them to the movies. Just the ice cream. And some Xbox games. That's a good night. And pizza. Don't forget the pizza.

Do you even have movie theaters up there?

I believe you're Santa. I really do. I never told anyone that wish. Not even my uncle.

I'd like to come work at the North Pole one day. Do I need to give you my resume or something? That's what they call it, rite? A resume. My mom said it's French for continuing your career. Like resuming it. Not sure that's true but she always sounds sure of herself when she says stuff like that.

My dad doesn't talk much any more with my uncle dead. They were brothers you know. Uncle Kevin was his baby brother, my mom says. It's weird to think of a grown up as a baby to anyone but I can hear my dad crying like a baby late at night downstairs when he thinks we're all asleep. My mom says he needs time. It sounds like he's going to need a whole lot of time. Whatever that means.

My friend from down the street Tiffany Bullock said I should use a weegee board to try to talk to my uncle. She's in fifth grade so she's a little older than me and she said she tried to use one to talk to her mom after she died. She didn't say whether it worked or not but I want to try whatever gets the job done, you know what I mean?

I should probly go now. I don't know what else to say rite now.

Christmas is coming soon. You're probably reely busy rite now. I hope the elfs feel better soon.

Pen pals for life.

Your frend,

Emily A.

PWB

19th of December

Dear Emily,

I am so very sorry about your uncle. It sounds as if he was a second father to you and I know that hurts so much more than a young person such as yourself should be allowed to withstand.

I need you to understand what I'm about to say very clearly. Understood? Whatever you do, please DO NOT use a "weegee" board to try to talk to your uncle. They are unbelievably bad news and I don't want you getting mixed up in anything scary or dangerous. I found one of my elfs, one of the assistant managers in the video games department, Jean, with a "weegee" board in his chambers a few months ago. Of course, I made him get rid of it right away. You should do the same and tell your friend in fifth grade Tiffany Bullock to stay away from such stuff as well if she wants that iPad she's been so vocal about lately. Please tell me you understand. It is for your own good. There are other ways to let your uncle know you miss him. I promise.

You are right, my dear. Christmas is almost here and it will be even closer by the time you get this new letter!

I don't want to alarm you or anything, but the blizzards are getting more and more frequent this year and much more violent. A few days ago, we lost a few of the reindeer when the southern stables collapsed under the weight of all this blasted snow. A few more ran into the pine barrens north of my compound, startled by the destruction. Most of the elfs refused to go there to retrieve them. I had to go myself with the help of only one companion, a brave little fellow named Randolph. One of the janitors. He makes a great mug of hot chocolate, too. When we returned from that harrowing (that means scary) place with the reindeers in tow, he soon started babbling about something hiding in the trees. Even the reindeer wouldn't go near him from then on. I had him moved into one of my guest bungalows so he would not frighten the other elfs at night with his incessant gibberish (that's like creepy nonsense talk). But Mrs. Claus' patience is wearing thin with him. I'm not sure how much longer I can keep him there. Our resident therapist is on vacation and our medical staff says there's nothing physically wrong with him. He is most certainly scaring me a bit though; I have to admit. Does it surprise you to know Santa can get scared? Is there anything that scares you? We can swap scaredy cat secrets! Ha!

I hope this isn't all too much for you to read, my new pen pal. I just need a calm voice to bounce things off of – you know what I mean?

PWB and I'll tell you what I mean about your uncle and how you can still talk to him the right way. Not the dangerous way. Sound good?

Your pen pal for life,

Mr. C

P.S.: PWB Soon

January 2

Dear Santa,

I'm not to sure about everything you said to be onest. I had to google a lot of those words. I didn't use the weegee board after all. It gave me the heebie jeebies just looking at it. I checked one of your letters to make sure I knew how to spell heebie jeebies the rite way. Tiffany said she used it a few times and now she hears loud thumping in the attic when she can't sleep at night wich is apparently most nights. I don't like the sound of that so I said I can't come over to her place any more. At least not for sleepovers.

I'm sorry about your reindeer. We lost our family dog Sniffers a couple of years ago and I still miss him. He didn't help deliver toys or anything like that but he was a good cuddler and didn't mind eating my peas when they showed up on my dinner plate.

That place you had to go to sounds bad. I wouldn't want to end up there for all the money in the world. I think that's a bunch. More than a bunch.

You can tell me anything you feel okay with telling me. I'm good at keeping secrits. If you're scared and sad, just think of me and my poleroid. We can do a super cool photo shoot some day when I work for you. The elfs and the reindeers and Mrs. Claus can be in it to. I can't wait for it to be real.

I hope you had a good Christmas. I'm sure you already knew I didn't need anything because I didn't see anything from you under the tree. I mean, my parents got me a new laptop and said it was from you but I could tell it was all them. Its cute they still do that. I know when it's really you. Especially now that we're pen pals for life.

Bringing up Sniffers makes me miss my uncle even more. It hurts so much. When do you think it gets better? Have you lost someone like my Uncle Kevin? Do you have any advice what to do to make it better?

Tell me you're okay and I'll feel better. A few kids down my street said they didn't get anything from you either. Did you send them their gifts early also? Are you getting lazey or are robots doing everything ahed of time now?

PWB.

Your no weegee using pen pal for life,

Emily A.

16th of January

My Dear Emily,

They're all dead.

My beloved wife, Mrs. Claus. The reindeer. All of my human employees, including several international kid representatives from around the world. Most of my elfs. Gone.

I don't have much more time, my dear sweet Emily.

Shortly after I sent you my last letter all Hell broke loose. I'm sorry for swearing, but that's exactly what happened.

Those things…

They came from the barrens north of us. The elfs. My poor, sweet elfs. They were using spirit boards and occult manuscripts to contact the dead. To try to predict what children might want for future Christmases. A way of improving efficiency. I would applaud their ingenuity if it weren't so horrifyingly reckless. Oh how I wish they had asked me first. Then all of this could have been…

There's no time for that now. No time to pity the foolish dead. That comes later.

The elfs wakened something truly not of this world with their well-meaning meddling. I cannot even begin to describe those ungodly things. How they appeared to us out of the northern blackness. Their wretched stench. Tendrils and teeth. Shadows and emptiness. They murmured and chattered and jabbered all the while as they tore my friends and family to ribbons. There's blood everywhere. I slipped on it several times trying to escape their wrath. I tried to fight back, but my magic weakens severely amongst such death and hopelessness.

I'm locked in the utility closet at the east end of the manufacturing plant. I can hear them scurrying around, looking for me and any remaining elfs loyal to me. Loyal to the living. To the Light.

I sent brave Sebastian, my elfish personal assistant, to mail these letters to my closest child confidants. Kids like you. Brave souls and kindred spirits to me and all I hold dear. There are not many of you out there and you are chief among them, Emily. You must follow the instructions I have included with this letter *exactly* in order to find your way here to the North Pole and save me. Your pure goodness can help turn the tide and fight back this horrific evil that has been unleashed upon us. I am so sorry to have to ask this of you but now it's the only way Christmas can have a chance of surviving at all.

I do not expect Sebastian to return. Such a brave soul. I will never forget his actions this day.

If I don't see you and the others soon, I'll assume Sebastian was slain on his way to the mailbox or you have read this letter and decided it was too dangerous to come aid me. I do not blame you if so. Live your life to the fullest and stay far, far away from this accursed place.

If you deem the journey to be worthy, in the name of all that is holy, please hurry.

Your pen pal for life and friend to the end,

Mr. C

YouTube clip from the local newscast in Stafford County, Virginia - 1/30/24

A young male anchor adorned in a blue parka with the hood off and his coiffed hair lightly miffed in the cold breeze of late January in Northern Virginia. Identified as Parker Gingold on the chyron graphic at the bottom of the video. WABC-TV Nightly News.

"I'm coming to you live now from the gated housing community of Aquia Harbor where a young girl has gone missing from her neighborhood for nearly a week now. Ten-year-old Emily Adams vanished without a trace shortly after her tenth birthday. Her parents provided authorities with a series of letters from someone claiming to be Santa Claus himself. A disturbing letter writing relationship seemingly developed between Emily and her possible groomer. A cryptic note left with the suspect's last letter apparently gave instructions on how to find him and his alleged lair. Local police turned up nothing upon following the trail. Emily's disappearance marks the seventh potential abduction tied to a series of letters from someone posing as Santa Claus in as many different states as well as one in the United Kingdom and two in Southeast Asia. This tragic case is very much still developing and we will be there for any breakthroughs. Back to you in the studio, guys."

Near the end of the video, something else remains...

The coverage returns to the news studio and away from Parker Gingold. At the desk are two anchors, a curly-locked young woman with an effervescent smile and a grizzled veteran newscaster of an older man.

The woman, Tina Truesdale, speaks first.

"Thanks, Parker. What a nightmare of a story. Can you imagine? Some awful human being posing as Santa Claus of all things just to lure little kids to a horrible fate. I just can't believe it. I don't think I want to believe it. Cal?"

The man, Cal Russo, clears his throat and picks up from where Tina left off with a grim, bothered tone.

"In world news, a contingent of Finnish and Russian firefighters are reported to have responded to the apparent forest fire in the North Pole, as it were. Finnish officials claim the brilliant crimson red northern lights currently visible in the atmosphere are the result of a large and dangerous pine tree wildfire threatening to alter the climate of the country itself. Varangerhalvoya National Park in Finland is the approximate location to be more specific. The event has baffled many in the scientific community, especially those who have asked for permission to investigate the phenomena and were denied access. When asked for further comment on why firefighters would be called to a virtual frozen tundra, a spokesperson for the Finnish department of the Interior simply stated, "there is more up there than just snow. That national park is a treasure to us and contains many things outsiders would simply not understand. We are working tirelessly to protect our precious resources from potential destruction." As always, we'll follow this bizarre turn of events as it continues to develop."

Tina still has her same painted on smile as she takes over.

"Thanks, Cal. What a weird way to say your country has global warming. I mean, we're all dealing with climate change, am I right? Up next, the sports roundup with Gary Dickerson. We'll be right back."

PART & PARCEL

"Fuck Christmas in its stupid ass," Miles Flint mumbled as he exhaled in utter defeat.

The fickle cold weather of December in Central Virginia had decided to rear its ugly head that week with a wet, bitter cavalcade of seasonal depression. It only exacerbated the broken nose and bruised jaw he now sported thanks to Miriam. His wife had never struck him before. Not even a hint of violence from her for nearly twenty years of complacent wedded bliss. But on that night, she lashed out. Hard. Twice. Miles wasn't sure if it was because of what he had said to her, or to their kids, or both barely an hour ago but whatever did the trick, it was the proverbial last straw.

"Don't come back in this house unless you have a god damn job and you apologize to Santa Claus!"

Those shrill, stinging words lingered in his ears with a burning numbness. He had indeed told his kids there was no Santa Claus and had also indeed told his wife, a dyed-in-the-wool Christmas fanatic, that he hated Christmas. Hated it with a fiery passion.

"I fucking hate Christmas, babe." Those were his exact words.

Those two punches to the face delivered by Miriam hurt less than her pegging him as a loser. A layabout. A bad husband. A shitty father.

The weak glow of the busted neon sign above Albie's Liquor Store mocked him and his every thought. Every move. Every time he took a swig of the knockoff Bacardi ensconced in the brown paper bag he was death-gripping in his left hand, the one with the constant reminder known as his wedding band, he could feel the red and yellow sign judging him. Writing him off.

Your wife tells you to get your shit together and you come to me in all my glory. You can't afford to buy your kids even the cheapest gifts, but you got enough scratch for a bottle of shitty booze. Drink up, loser.

In his right hand was his phone, with which he was currently doomscrolling social media. Facebook, Twitter, Instagram, TikTok, back and forth all at once.

A wet, scruffy, and severely layered bum walked in front of his car, really his wife's car, and pissed on the façade belonging to Albie's. Like weak rain on weak metal siding from inside the relative safety of the vehicle. After the bum finished micturating upside the liquor store, he took one look at Miles through the rain-slicked windshield and clicked his teeth.

"The fuck you looking at, shitbird?" asked the bum with a firm degree of annoyance.

Disrespected by strangers on top of everything else. It was enough to drive someone to suicide at a time such as this. But Miles was too lazy to even do that right. So, he just waved at the bum and swigged another swig of the barrel-bottom rum he hastily purchased barely moments ago inside good ol' Albie's.

"Get a fuckin' job, asshole," the bum said dismissively as he shuffled off to find a better place to shit, Miles surmised.

As he doomscrolled and drank, the bum's words burrowed deeper and deeper into his very being.

Get a fuckin' job, asshole.

Was that really the solution? To everything? Nothing's that easy. Or is it?

Damn it all to hell.

Ceasing his relentless scroll of doom, Miles ejected from the social media cockpit and brought Reddit up on his phone. He navigated to a subreddit he frequented late at night.

r/Odd Jobs & Odd Shit

Fuck. Here goes nothing.

Amidst all the postings of would-be porn shoots and bizarre gig economy lifestyle photos, there was a single post that both revolted and captivated him.

Crone Industries Hiring Mall Santas. $30/hr. Don't have to be fat. Must pass thorough testing. Call 800-555-1468.

"Huh."

The ad initially made him want to chuck his phone out the window. Mall Santas? Didn't they know Miles hated Christmas? With a fiery passion, to be exact. Parental divorce, near poverty, capitalistic fetishism, religious nonsense. All flags Miles burned long ago. Until he met Miriam. She was into fucking to Christmas music all year round. But she was drop dead gorgeous and very accommodating to all his baggage and bullshit. So, he lied and said he was all on board with the holiday. Thanksgiving and New Year's, too. Just to be safe.

Two kids and seventeen years later and he just couldn't take it anymore. It was barely a month until Christmas and Miriam had the egg nogg out already, flipping through her vinyl Xmas collection. What was it going to be tonight? Bing? Nat? The god damn Peanuts? It was too much for him to take so soon after the passing of his mother over the summer. She was the last bastion of his youth. Now he was just another Gen X asshole, adrift in a sea of suburbia and marking time until his genetic replacements cause a widowmaker finale in his already shriveled heart. He didn't hate his kids, though. It was just having to be around them that bothered him. He loved the *idea* of kids and goofing around with them, but that was where it ended. He was solid uncle material that fooled himself into thinking he was dad material.

All of that was swirling around in his head when he blurted out how much he hated Christmas just as Miriam was about to spin Burl Ives on the turntable. It stopped her in her tracks so hard you would have thought *she* was the one about to bite it from an infarction. As she stood there, stunned; the kids, Noel and Nick, ten-year-old fraternal twins on top of it all, scooted in to see what all the commotion was about. And that's when it happened. Just seeing their faces, their little brains waiting for Daddy to apologize or to say everything was alright. It broke him. It made him scuttle with anger and bitterness throughout his entire being.

"There's no fucking Santa Claus and Christmas can suck my fucking dick."

He couldn't even recall what their faces looked like after he let loose that verbal volley, but mostly because Miriam had regained mobility and clarity and delivered two punches right to his face. Jaw and nose. Painful and even more painful, one right after the other. Her ring hand.

But that ad also enticed the hell out of him, even if he was loathe to admit it. Thirty bucks an hour was nothing to sneeze at for seasonal work. Especially for someone without current employment. No Santa gut required. Miles checked that box with authority. Testing? What kind of damn testing? IQ test? Obstacle course? Even if he wasn't psyched about schlepping around a mall food court trailed by a gaggle of piss-stained toddlers, the whole testing thing intrigued him to no end.

He had to make a call. Bo would know what to do.

He searched for Bo's number in his call history and rang him up. A couple ring-a-lings later and Bo answered in his husky growl of a voice.

"Hey man. What… Uh, what's up?"

Was he indisposed? Damn it, always the wrong time to call. Everyone texted nowadays. Miles hated texting almost as much as Christmas.

"Yo, Bo! What's the haps? It's your boy."

"Yeah, I know who it is man. As I said, what's up?"

Bo was Miles' oldest friend. They started hanging out around the same time Miles met Miriam. So, he was more than up to date on everything in that department. Lately, though, Miles and Bo had started to grow distant as Bo, a lifetime confirmed bachelor, was starting to catch pangs of love and marriage more and more frequently. Getting close to fifty will do that to some guys, apparently.

"Are you, uh… With somebody?"

"Mmhmm."

"Look, I uh, I just needed to talk to—"

"She kicked you out again, huh?"

"Well, I think I kinda deserved it this time."

There was then the sound of Bo dropping his phone straight to the ground followed by frantic fumbling to retrieve it.

"You there?"

"You finally did it! Holy shit. Dude we've been talking about this forever. You showed her your true self, man. I'm proud of you."

"Well, I'm not sure I dig my true self if that's the case. I yelled at my kids, man. You know that kills me every time I do it. Like I really let them have it."

"They're brats. Miriam made sure of that. And your unwillingness to do anything about it didn't help, either. Time for the big D-word now, my man. You've earned it."

Bo's words stuck in Miles' gut and spawned a million butterflies. Did he really want that? It was so final. He still loved M. Just not her stupid holiday fetish. He loved his kids. When they were away from *her*. Damn it. Human relationships were so frigging complicated. No such thing as just ripping off a Band-Aid when it came to familial tomfoolery.

"I still love 'em, man."

And that's when Bo hung up.

"Yo. Bo? Fuuuuuuck…"

Divorce or the Santa suit. Freedom or the continued psychological damage to his kids, but with continued hot sex with his insane wife.

Decisions, decisions.

That same bum was coming back around the corner of the liquor store and already eyeing Miles. Miles quickly dialed the number from the ad, gritting his teeth. Someone picked up at once, which startled him into a temporary stupor.

"*Age, weight,*" the low, crinkly voice on the other end demanded.

Miles almost blanked but regained his composure just as the voice was about to ask again, this time more forcefully he wagered.

"Forty-five. About a hundred-ninety pounds."

"*Height.*"

"Six foot. Wait. In shoes or no shoes?"

"*Be at the following address in one hour. 1200 Austria Way. Crone Industries. Park by the side entrance. Do not be late.*"

"Yes, and thank—"

Another phone hung up on him. The night itself was imposing an unappetizing theme right on top of Miles whether he approved or not. As he turned the key to the ignition, he wondered if he could actually go through with killing himself if he didn't get this job.

Merry fucking Christmas, Miles.

* * *

Crone Industries would never be mistaken for a lair of festivity or a cradle of mall Santas or *anything* of the sort. No red or green to be seen for miles. It was just another industrial megalith structure amidst a sea of industrial megalith structures on the side of town Miles and people like him actively avoided. Loading bay doors, towering chimneys, a crumbling brick façade,

115

and a massive, empty parking lot completed the latter-day industry ensemble.

Miles had parked on the right side of the building, which thoroughly irked him as said massive parking lot was indeed bone dry and emptier than his bank account. Both checking and savings. Why the side? There wasn't even a parking lot there. He was just idling next to a shoddy metal door hilariously covered by a tattered cloth awning that looked ready to just lay down and die any day now. It wasn't even festive. Just a faded cream and brown pattern. Gross and dated. Miles couldn't stop staring at it as it was the only movement in the immediate area. Lifelessness permeated this block the same way Christmas permeated the Flint household year-round. Well, moreso the Cole household, as Miriam kept her last name and insisted the kids keep it too. Probably smart in the long run, considering the night's events, Miles admitted to himself.

Whether he wanted to muse more on how screwed his life was or not, a figure emerged from the creaky, rusty metal side door. An elderly man with a wild whisp of white hair that caught the wind as soon as it was outside in the open, sending it straight up in the air and making Miles snicker if ever so slightly. The man was wrapped in a tight, thick, and long wool trench coat with the collar standing straight up. At first, he just stood there, staring at Miles with empty eyes and barely an expression of impatience on his wrinkled visage.

Then, as Miles registered that the man was waiting on him to exit the car and come to *him*, he gave Miles a slight wave. The absolute slightest of wave. No arm movement, just a flourish of his hand out of his pocket and then right back into the pocket. Almost imperceptible if you were further away than where Miles was parked.

Okay then. Time to save my marriage.

It sounded corny as all get out in Miles' head, but he decided that's *exactly* what he was doing. He was sure this would fix everything once and for all.

As he got out of his car (his wife's car, really) a violent, repugnant stench of rotting meat and sour milk assaulted his nose without mercy. It sent him staggering and he looked at the old man in the massive trench coat to see if he was smelling it, too. If he was, his poker face was supreme and absolute.

What the hell…

"This way, young man…" The man with the wispy head of hair intoned hoarsely to Miles. If it wasn't already freezing out, the man's voice would send a solid shiver up his spine. Before he was even up the steps, the old man had returned inside. The gust of rot had dissipated, and Miles could feel the warmth of indoor heating squeeze out as the metal door clanged shut in front of him.

"Don't worry, I got the door, thanks," Miles said under his breath, but just loud enough he hoped the old jerk had heard him.

Inside, Miles was greeted by labyrinthine corridors of worn lime green walls. No front desk, no office. Just hallways upon hallways.

"Down this way, young man…"

Indoors, the old man's echoing voice had a Germanic bent to it. Bavarian? Austrian? Swiss? It was hard to say.

"I'm sorry, where exactly?" Miles called out to a long, almost glow-in-the-dark hall.

"Follow my voice," the old man said, his tone raising significantly.

It was coming from the end of the hall he was in and to the immediate left. So, Miles followed his instinct and made his way down the absurdly long corridor. No pictures, no certificates, signs, or anything of that sort on the walls whatsoever. Just bare acreage blanketed in weak fluorescent light.

Though the old man's voice had a distinct echo, Miles' footsteps did not. The sound of his footfalls down the hall died just as quickly as they were born. It felt as if anything at all could sneak up on him from anywhere, even right in front of his face.

"Not very festive in here, is it?" Miles chuckled, trying to be conversational as best he could, given the little he had to go off.

No answer back from the wispy-haired trench coat man, but as Miles turned the corner to where he surmised the man's voice was coming from, there he was. Literally right around the corner, standing quite still. Another step or two and Miles would have run smack into him.

That stench of rot had returned a smidge and caused Miles to scrunch up his face in a vain attempt to be rid of it.

"Sorry. My bad. I—"

The old man's eyes were fixed on Miles. Unblinking. Nearly black. He had a slight lip twitch that was making Miles just as nauseous as the rotting smell.

"Right down that way, young man." His breath was horrible, but it wasn't where the rotting smell was coming from. Just gingivitis and halitosis there.

The old man was signaling with an outstretched arm to a door about halfway down the current hall they were in. Still lime green and all sorts of faded. But the door was red. Bright red. Fire engine red. It was the first sign of the holiday at hand he had seen in this place yet. As much as he hated Christmas, or "Xmas" as he insisted on referring to it as, he was glad to see this festive portal of potential possibilities.

"She will see you now."

The old man didn't move a muscle. But his eyes were still locked onto Miles. Not a blink in sight.

"...Okay, then. Nice meeting you."

Miles headed for the door, head tingling knowing the man's eyes were most likely still on him all the way. As he reached the red door, he turned to glance back at the old man, hoping to see a smile or even a dismissive wave. Something decidedly not creepy.

"By the way, didn't catch your name—"

The man was gone. It spooked Miles a large amount until he realized all the guy had to do was take a few steps around the corner. But then the thought of the old wispy-haired man leering at him from behind a dark hallway corner spooked him even more. As he turned the handle to the door, he had a mild panic attack that something would grab him from behind just as he entered the perceived safety of that bright shiny, red door. But nothing came. Miles couldn't decide whether or not that was even scarier.

There *was* an actual office on the other side of that door. A nice one to boot. Nothing at all resembling the nightmare maze of paranoia-inducing corridors he was just in or the oppressive industrial façade outside. This was downright corporate. Cheery, even. A cluster of chairs in the center of the room signified the waiting area and next to that was a water cooler, a coffee machine and a tray of Christmas cookies on a folding table. Looked like gingerbread. Smelled like it, too. Framed posters of old school holiday shenanigans out of some Norman Rockwell/Coca-Cola merger no one ever made public. The receptionist desk held no receptionist that Miles could see. After a few moments of looking around, he decided to grab a coffee, avoid the cookies, and pop a squat in one of the barely cushioned hardback chairs. Someone *should* be with him shortly. They had to be. No one else was around. Unless there was a thorough interview going on right now with some other down-and-out bloke. How long would that take? Testing. Testing. Testing. What did that really mean? Miles assumed he was about to find out.

* * *

Three hours later, he still hadn't found out. Not even an intercom announcement. Two cups of coffee, a cup of water, and a bite of the accursed gingerbread later, and still nothing. He had threatened to himself to get up and leave at least eight times over the last two of those three hours. But leave to go where? Return to what? Domestic life for Miles was in shambles to put it mildly. Maybe this was all a test? How long can you stand to wait to get signed for thirty bucks an hour and all the mall food court Chinese you can eat?

As he was about to reluctantly vacate the relative safety of the strange office for real this time, the sound of a door clunking open somewhere behind the receptionist desk made him flinch. Someone was coming. Finally. Was it the wispy-haired trench coat of a man? No. He said *she* would see him now. Now meaning hours later, of course. Who could it be—

And then she appeared, heels clicking on the hardwood floor. All business. Horn-rimmed glasses, starched blouse with a sleek choker around her sloping neck, pleated knee-length skirt adorning long yet stocky legs. Dirty blond hair tied up at the top of her head, creating a fountain of cascading curls. Freckled cheeks, deep red lipstick and no eyeliner or mascara to speak of. He couldn't help but stare. Was this his supervisor? The owner of his place? He had so many questions and before his brain could ask another one, she had extended her hand out to him quite pleasantly. Her demeanor was a confident mix of business and casual. He wasn't sure if he should shake her hand or hug her.

Don't hug her, dummy.

And she smelled of Christmas. Not secular, store-bought Christmas. Old world, traditional-as-fuck Christmas. Almost Pagan-esque. Miles wasn't sure exactly what the ingredients of such a thing would even be, but he knew that was it.

"Good evening. I am Perdita Engel. But you can call me Frau Perdita or just Frau if you like. Thank you for coming in to be evaluated," she said as she smiled at him all the while.

"...Evaluated?"

"Yes for the shopping mall Santa Claus position."

Her words had a distinct German or Austrian accent to them, even more so than the old man. The way she pronounced Santa Claus gave him the tingles.

Sinta Klauz

Clawing out of his mild bemusement and her unexpected beauty in a place like this, Miles attempted to sound like a lucid human being.

"Oh, yes. Yes, thank you for seeing me. I'm very much looking forward to potentially fitting the bill."

"Are you?"

Her tone changed just slightly. Now it was inquisitive in nature. Or was that sarcasm?

"Yes... Yes I am," he said as he regained his composure with a straightening of his back and a slight grin.

"Good. It's hard to find candidates that meet our exact criteria. Hence the late posting. Usually, we have someone by now."

"No one wants to work anymore, am I right?" Miles put his hands on his hips and chuckled, hoping to get a laugh.

"Especially you, Mr. Flint, yes?"

What?

"I'm sorry? How did you—"

You just told it to me when we shook hands.

"I did?"

"Yes. You did."

"Oh. Sorry, I'm just having a really bad night. Please excuse me."

"Not at all. It is quite alright. Shall we begin?"

"In here? Or…"

"Follow me, young man," she said as she returned to the door she had just appeared from.

"Okay."

Miles was flummoxed. Did he tell her his name or not? How did she see through his humorous attempt to mask his rampant joblessness? It was all weird all over, but not enough to thumb his nose at thirty bucks an hour and hot tub sex with his wife again. Oh, and seeing his kids again. That too.

*　*　*

She took him to a stark white room with just one feature inside. A large, grey cushioned examination table that would look at home in any random doctor's office. No chairs, no other tables. Just the harsh light coming from overhead.

"Please, take a seat on the table."

After a few long seconds of hesitation, more for effect than anything, Miles made his way over to it and scooted up there, making deep squeaky sounds all the while. He wanted to make an innocent fart joke to break the silence that had come over them, but he realized at the last second that ideas of that sort were probably why he was perpetually unemployed.

"I am going to examine you for the pre-employment physical. While I do this, I will ask you questions about your health history and psychological state. Are you okay with such things?"

"Uh, yeah. I mean, yes. It's perfectly okay with me."

Don't be a pervert. Don't be a pervert. Don't be a—

Her firm hand began to palpate his sides, his back, his neck, his thighs. She was stronger than she looked, but not forceful in any way. He kind of liked it. Not exactly a massage, but some kind of human touch, nonetheless.

"Any of these things sore or sensitive to touch?"

"No."

"Good. I will now check your breathing."

She pulled out a stethoscope and placed it on his chest.

"Just breathe in and out with regularity, yes?"

"Sure."

As he breathed and while she kept the stethoscope there, her voice lowered a bit and became more serious in nature as opposed to the more jovial lilt she had kept so far.

"You seem to be in good weight. Have you ever been fat in your life, Mr. Flint?"

Huh?

"Well, I had a little extra chub in elementary school. But that's about it. Baby fat I guess?"

"Were you bullied for it?"

"What?"

"Where you bullied for your... baby fatness?"

"Uh, no. Not really. Hard to remember that far back."

"These are yes or no questions, Mr. Flint."

"No, I guess. Yeah, no."

"Hm."

She moved her stethoscope to his back.

"Continue to breathe in a normal fashion, yes?"

"Okay."

A couple quiet inhales and exhales transpired before she spoke again.

"Have you ever participated in binge eating?"

"Excuse me?"

"Consuming food until your stomach is so full, it becomes painful until you digest it."

"Sometimes, yeah. I mean, yes. Like Thanksgiving or Christmas. Stuff like that."

"No bulimia or anorexia?"

Why would she ask a guy that? Weren't those female diseases? This was getting too weird, even for thirty bucks an hour.

"I'm sorry, what does that have to do with being a mall Santa?"

"Crone Industries has created the most efficient method of determining suitable candidates. Please bear with us as I finish our patented evaluations. Yes?"

Thirty bucks an hour. Mall food court Chinese. Fix your family. Sex with Miriam. Kids and stuff.

"Sure, sure. Sorry."

"It is quite alright. Most men ask these same things. It is understandable."

"No women Santas?"

"Mrs. Claus auditions are uptown, Mr. Flint. Much nicer facility."

"Ah. I see."

Was that misandry in her tone? Miles tried to put it out of his mind lest his mouth get him in trouble again tonight. Twice was enough.

One final question for now, Mr. Flint.

"Sure. Shoot."

"What does Christmas mean to you?"

Oh no.

"Uh…"

Miles knew right then the interview was fucked beyond repair. He couldn't lie. She seemed to be able to tell when that shit happened. What if he told her the truth? His hatred of Christmas and how he was doing this for his family and to bring them back together despite how much it would pain him to don that suit, but it would be worth it in the long run because he wanted to be a good dad and a loving husband with gainful employment. Maybe this could lead to more jobs in between holiday seasons? The possibilities seemed endless in that span of mere seconds.

Yeah, just tell her the truth.

And so, he did. He told her all about the entire night up to this point and how he felt about *everything*. He came close to breaking down in tears. Not because of anything he mentioned, but because he thought it would help if he remembered his beagle Skipper dying when he was eleven and how those tears would seal the deal and get the job for him.

After he finished speaking for nearly five minutes straight, talking mostly to the floor and fidgeting with his hands, he looked up at Frau Perdita and almost did a double take. She was staring right at him with nary a blink, much akin to her old man co-worker. It unnerved Miles. She was looking through him, inside him, around him, feeling him out with her eyeballs. Rubbing them on his organs, making his skin crawl and his brain throb. He had a momentary burst of panic, spurring him to escape that place once and for all, but it disappeared as soon as she spoke again. He liked her voice *a lot* for some reason.

Think of Miriam. Miriam. Miriam. Miriam. Hot tub sex. Hell, even Christmas music during said hot tub sex.

"I appreciate you telling me all of this, Mr. Flint. I think we have a position for you here at Crone Industries."

Miles was flabbergasted. It worked. His bullshit actually worked. Miriam hardly ever went for it these days. It was so refreshing to get validation from a relative stranger. But she didn't feel strange anymore. She felt warm, inviting. That old world holiday smell clicked for him. Fresh poinsettias and piping hot spice bread; it was intoxicating to him now.

"You do? I mean, you do? Really?"

"Yes, of course. Thank you for your candor, Miles. It is so refreshing to hear such a thing especially at this time of year."

"Oh. Th-thank you. Thanks."

He smiled a little too much and extended his hand for a celebratory shake.

She didn't return it.

"Please wait here. I will return shortly with your paperwork, yes?"

"O-okay, sure. In for a penny, in for a pound. What's another hour now anyways, right?"

Miles let a laugh loose in the room that seemed to bounce around several times before falling flat on its face in embarrassment. Frau Perdita still didn't laugh or smile back. She just nodded and made for the door. Was he too overeager in his triumph? Was she going to return with a cease and desist or a restraining order? Something that would forever destroy his night and his life permanently? How could he go back to Miriam and the kids with nothing but a tall tale to tell of his experience here? They'd never even believe—

Before he could finish that banal thought, the wispy-haired old man in the thick trench coat marched through the door and came straight for Miles. He wasn't smiling either. As a long, outstretched arm neared Miles, the old man's mouth opened wide and revealed a black abyss of yawning hunger. Groans and shrieks of all kinds seemed to emanate directly from it. Miles involuntarily squealed and tried to eject himself from the sticky fabric of the examination table, but the blackness took him before the fear even fully registered in his brain.

The smells...

Cranberry sauce... Stuffing... Honey ham... Turkey gravy... Mashed potatoes with butter... Butternut squash... The scents utterly pervaded his nostrils, and he had a crude picture in his mind of where he might be before he even opened his eyes.

And then he did.

A dining room. But not his own. Not Miriam's. No. This one was different. It was the most festive, holiday-themed dining room he had ever laid eyes on. Garland and tinsel and poinsettias and wreaths everywhere along with a massive, ten-foot-tall Christmas tree in the far corner by the door. The only actual door he could see in this abomination of a chamber. Miriam had a flair for this kind of thing for sure, but this here was light years beyond anything she had ever attempted. It would probably be her ultimate sexual fantasy come true.

But it was where Miles was *seated* that truly sent his brain into terror mode.

A huge, mahogany dining table that could chair about sixteen people easily. He was placed to the left of the head of the table. A gargantuan plate of holiday meal fixings sat in front him, untouched. Heat wafting off it as if it had just been placed there. Maybe that's what woke him?

But that wasn't all.

He wasn't alone.

Across from him and one chair over, was a corpse. Miles was sure in that moment the guy was dead. His eyes still open, but his mouth locked in a death frown that was unmistakable. Glasses rested askew on his twisted brow, a waxed handlebar mustache peppered with crumbs of food from his nearly finished plate, which looked as if had been just as massive as Miles' judging from the dish size and the gloppy remnants of the meal itself. The man's hands were frozen stiff, clawing at his distended, bloated stomach which had burst through his pinstriped dress shirt and looked black and blue and purple with bruises and stretch marks.

"What the—"

"He… couldn't… finish…"

A weak, exhausted man's voice broke Miles out of his state of shock. It was coming from the far side of the table, at the other head. Or foot? Miles could never remember proper dining etiquette. A relic of old times no one cared to cherish anymore.

Miles turned his groggy head to meet the voice and sure enough, there was a man seated at exactly that location. Scraggly beard, angular face. He looked to be as thin and wiry as Miles, save for his massive belly that appeared as distended and swollen as the dead man across from Miles. He too was clawing at it his stomach in agony, trying to soothe something that clearly couldn't be soothed at this point.

"What the hell is… Where are we?"

"It's… the… final part of the… Ughh…. Ahhhhhh!"

The man was clearly in the worst pain a human could possibly be in. Pregnancy seemed hilarious compared to the look on this man's face, Miles decided. Was there some*thing* trying to get out? Had this turned into some sort of horrific lab experiment to breed some kind of mutant messiah child on Christmas or something? Miles' mind raced with all the depraved possibilities.

"I can't… You have to… Final part of the interview… Ohhhh Goddddd…"

And with that, the man's stomach stretched another inch or two with a sick, fleshy squeeze, and then it popped. Sounded just like a balloon. So much so that Miles didn't even fully process what was actually happening until the man's blood and intestinal chunks had reached his end of the table. They were in his plate of food, on his face, and in his eyes. Whatever they had drugged him with delayed his reaction time to the point of near inaction. He couldn't even gag or wretch or vomit in response to the explosion. The room now smelled of stomach acid and saliva-infused mashed potatoes.

"I didn't make itttt… Youuuu have to finishhhhhh ittt alllll…" The man practically whispered as the last ounce of his lifeforce left his ravaged body.

Finish it all? That was impossible. Especially now that it was garnished with that guy's innards.

No fucking way. Interview over, godammit.
"Uhhhhh…" Was all Miles could muster to an overly jolly room of dead men with no stomachs.

And then the door opened. The old man with the wispy hair was back. Miles flinched mentally in preparation for another taste of the guy's oral abyss, but it didn't come. The old man just stood there, still as a stalk of corn in a breezeless field.

Behind him, a hideous, shriveled, ancient old woman entered the room. Warts, moles, whiskers, saggy skin, stretchy folds, oodles of liver spots everywhere. She was virtually a crone.

Crone. Crone Industries? The hell…?
The stench of rotting meat and milk had returned. Now Miles was certain it was coming from her. It had always been. Was she there all night, lurking, watching just out of sight? What shocked Miles more than

anything was that the crone was wearing the exact same outfit as Frau Perdita.

"Frau… Perdita? Is… is that you?"

"Frau Perchta. She will conduct the final portion of the interview now," Mr. Wisp said to Miles.

Perchta? The hell was that for a name?

"Begin to eat, Mr. Flint," the crone croaked as she approached him. Her clicking heels engaged in a much slower rhythm now.

Miles glanced again at his stomach-less companions with darting eyes. Flies had somehow found their way to both of them in this enclosed, windowless space.

"I'm not… hungry…"

Frau Perchta smiled, revealing her teeth. She still had all of them, but they were sharpened to a point and were yellow and grey all around. The rotting smell reached a crescendo as soon as she revealed them.

And that's when Miles puked. All over his food.

"Oh, that was very stupid, my boy. There are no more clean plates of food tonight. You must finish this meal that is in front of you as is."

"…What? I… I quit! I don't want the job!"

"Oh, my boy, you can't quit a job you don't have yet. And as you can see, our other candidates were… full of turkey, as the saying goes, yes? All talk and no stomach for such hard work."

Miles felt close to retching again as the crone laughed and clapped her hands excitedly.

"Eat!" The old man bellowed, threatening to hypnotize Miles with whatever was lurking in his mouth.

"Go easy on him. But not too easy, ha!" She chortled at the old man, who didn't even venture a smile or an easing of his stoic form.

"Pay no mind to Klaus. He is a stickler for tradition. If it were up to him, we would just eat you on sight. And that's no fun for anyone, is it?"

"Eat! Now!" The sound of old man Klaus' voice absolutely threatened another gaping abyss of unconsciousness and that terrified Miles.

So he ate.

Grabbing a fork in one hand and a knife in the other, Miles began to pile bite after bite into his mouth, ignoring the fact that his own puke and the man at the other end of the table's guts were smothered on top of all the otherwise delicious-looking food.

Merry fucking Christmas, Miles. Just think of Miriam. Hot tub sex. The kids I guess, too.

Gushy, gucky spoonful after mashed, moist, squishy spoonful went into Miles' mouth, and he was actually able to keep it down. This was it. His last chance to fix everything. It all made sense in the moment if not in a macro way. Miriam would forgive him, the kids wouldn't be scared of him anymore, and he'd be able to stand fucking to yuletide tunes until the cows came home. Maybe she'd be down for letting him ball her in the mall Santa suit. Another benefit of the job. He fantasized about coming back the next year, an MVP of the mall Santa scene. Welcomed back a hero. Appreciated. Loved. Maybe he could even get used to having a dad bod to fit the part more naturally. A nice little beer gut couldn't hurt.

Keep eating, Miles.

He could hear the crone's voice burrowing into his very psyche. He stopped for a moment and looked down. His belly was more than a little beer gut. It had distended and stretched well past the point of any kind of proportional normalcy. It was even well past the other man's point of explosion.

POP. POP. RRRRRIP.

His pants buttons and the fabric on his shirt gave way and his belly was firmly out there in the stale air of the jolly room. Jolly *prison* was more appropriate.

Holy shit.

How long had he been eating? Miles swore he had just started but his stomach said otherwise. He looked at his plate. It was almost licked clean save for a few more bites. Had the old man put him out again with his breath? His mouth? His whatever? Was Miles sleepeating? Was that even a thing?

"Excellent! You are doing so good, my boy. There'll be plenty of room for more than just straw and pebbles in that chamber of yours. Good work!"

Frau Perchta clapped excitedly again and croaked a series of laughs that resembled a family of sickly toads harmonizing with each other.

"Just a few more bites… Santa!"

Santa? Was that really who he was now? Yes! He had to be. After all of this, after what he told Perdita, his raw honesty. He was the ever-loving spirit of Christmas now! Miles excitedly polished off the last few bites of bloody squash and puke-covered stuffing.

"All done!" Miles said with a gushy mouthful.

"Yes, yes you are. And just in time, Miles."

The old man made a few quick strides over to Miles and pushed him backwards in his chair. He and the chair landed with a hard thud and then a **_CRRRACK_**. Miles knew he had broken the chair under his own newfound girth. But he didn't vomit. Not even a slight gag or reflux of food. Solid as a rock.

Santa material! That's me!

"What's this all about? I thought I passed. I'm Santa, right?"

The crone called Frau Perchta shuffled over to Miles, humming all the while, and as she slowly bent over to meet him face to face, the old man behind her procured a two-foot-long hunting knife from the bowels of his thick trench coat and handed it to her. Miles' eyes went wide, but he couldn't move a muscle. He was just too damn full. All he could do was breathe and blink and shift around barely an inch here and there. A marooned turtle or a cockroach unable to escape anything, let alone certain doom.

"There's no such thing as Santa Claus, Miles. Remember? You said so yourself. It's good to teach the kids that as soon as possible."

"…What? What—"

"I killed Santa Claus. Long ago. The only thing you should be thankful for on Christmas is that Frau Perchta doesn't pay you a visit. Not you as in directly you, of course. That ship has sailed, my boy. I mean more the royal you."

"Please… I—"

"You _are_ hired, though. Not as a mall Santa, mind you. But as a warning. A yearly message. You will send that message marvelously well, from the looks of it."

Without another word, the crone inserted the hunting knife directly above his groin and pushed in hard. It hurt more than anything he had experienced in his entire life, but the gluttony of his current state didn't allow much past just sitting there and taking it. And squealing a high-pitched whine of suffering.

"Merry fucking Christmas, as it were, Miles Flint."

And then she yanked the knife upwards, pulling his stomach wide open and spilling his guts to the floor with a liberal splash of hot, steaming blood. After that, she pulled his stomach out and handed it to Klaus, who promptly bit into it and began consuming the partially digested food with aplomb. Stomach acid and bile and smooshed food oozed from his mouth as grunty groans of satisfaction filled the room.

"The stomach is for him, yes, but I always love the guts. Intestines of those who pass the process really get me through the rest of the day. But considering you are our last interview for the year, this is merely my Christmas bonus, you might say. Yes?"

As Miles gives in to the heavy, black permanence of death, his last image his brain registers with any efficacy is that of the crone slurping on his crimson-coated intestines, steam billowing from her ravenous, chomping maw as her unblinking eyes burrowed into his vacating soul.

* * *

Miriam woke immediately from her deep slumber as soon as she heard the shocked cries of her children.

She hoped it wasn't Miles, drunk and passed out in a pile of puke on the living room floor. There was no explaining that one away anymore.

Besides, the asshole hadn't come around for weeks since that night. Showed his true fucking colors. Still, Miriam wished right then she had the foresight to change the locks to keep him from barging in at the most inopportune moments, like right now. Christmas Morning was sacred to her and by all rights sacred to her children. They weren't Miles' anymore, not after he revealed the real Miles in all his disgusting glory.

When she reached the bottom of the stairs, she saw right away what the kids had been wailing about. Miles was indeed there in the living room, but he wasn't passed out or covered in puke.

She was pretty sure he was dead.

Dressed in a Santa Claus suit and splayed out under the Christmas tree, squashing the presents she had so carefully selected for the kids. His stomach was gigantic, several feet stretched out with a hideous stitched scar running from below the navel up to his sternum. It all looked so painful, his belly poking out beyond obtrusiveness from his Santa jacket. On his bruised, stretched stomach skin, was scrawled the word **"NAUGHTY"** in a deep red substance. Blood?

"Daddy…?" Nick asked, a tremble in his voice.

Noel took a few steps back, almost tripping on the bottom stair.

"Wh…what's wrong with Dad—"

And that's right when Miles' stomach exploded.

Inside were all the gifts Miriam couldn't afford to get the kids. New smartphones, wireless headphones,

Nintendo Switches for both of them, gift cards to every store imaginable, candy out the wazoo, and so much more. Only a tiny bit of Miles' blood and guts were left in there so not too much of that sort of unpleasantness landed on Miriam and the kids' faces upon explosion. That was certainly considerate of Miles and his stomach.

Miriam would have been thankful for such a surprise Christmas miracle if her and the kids weren't screaming uncontrollably in abject terror.

AULD LANG STAB

[The following footage was recovered from 431 Rixeyville Court by the Powhatan County Sheriff's Office on January 3rd, 2022. What you are about to see was not edited to make the parties involved look worse than they already do. That's just the way they seem to be.]

[Brittany Mahaffey, a fortysomething prom queen who peaked in her late teens, holds her cell phone camera up to her face in selfie mode. Her mascara is tear-streaked and she wears a face of fear and panic.]

BRITTANY MAHAFFEY: Whoever finds this footage, in case we die here tonight, know that we tried to survive but the killers are still on the loose and we have no idea if we actually are going to live. So many are dead… So many—

[An impatiently annoyed voice cuts her off from in front of her, just off camera]

BRANDON MAHAFFEY: Babe. What the heck are you doing? Auditioning for The Amazing Race's Murder Dinner Theater? That's super-duper awful. No one's going to believe it. Just do the Blair Witch thing and we're golden.

[Between them are the bodies of a man and a woman. Stabbed to death. Callie and Micah Sorensen. They appear about the same age as Brittany and Brandon.]

BRITTANY: You're saying that like I know what you're talking about. Are you serious right now?

BRANDON: No, are *you* serious right now? You don't remember that Blair Witch movie? With all the shaky cam and the girl with the camera in her face with her runny nose saying how she misses her mommy?

BRITTANY: Oh. That movie. She was doing like a Survivor confessional or something.

BRANDON: Yes! Before Survivor was even a thing. Doesn't that blow your dang mind?

BRITTANY: Becca was watching that on TV last Halloween. I told her it would give her the tummy pukes after eating all that pizza and candy but does she listen to her mother? Ever?

BRANDON: She listens to me.

BRITTANY: You're not helping your standing with me currently.

BRANDON: Watch me, okay?

BRITTANY: Hey—

[Brandon grabs her phone and puts it to his face, uncomfortably close. He looks like a retired NFL quarterback who let himself go to a parodic level. He goes from annoyed dad face to weepy, doughy cry face in seconds flat.]

BRANDON: I don't know if we're going to make it… Oh God… Oh Jesus… Please, if you find this footage, don't stop looking for us. The killers are still inside the house. I think they're looking for us now. They're all dead… Callie and Micah, Daniel and Precious, Jenn and Simon, Brady and Bennett… All of them… We think Tom and Abby killed them all… We're all that's left… My wife is still alive here with me… We're trying to escape but please, if you can, get a message out to our kids… Becca, Freddie, Marcy, and Sammy. We love you guys… Mommy and Daddy love you… Oh God please help…

[Brandon hits stop on the phone's record button.]

[Brittany's phone cuts back on, recording again. Back in Brittany's hands.]

BRANDON: You have to edit all that out or people are gonna know what we did. Jeez, babe. Do you want me to help?

BRITTANY: Oh, I'm sorry, Mr. Laurence Olivier. Here's your Golden Globe for Best Lead Actor in a Comedy or Musical.

BRANDON: How do you know Laurence Olivier but not Blair Witch? That's one of the movies of our generation.

BRITTANY: I remember it now, Brand. Jeez Louise. Are you gonna hang that one over me for the next decade or what? I said I remember it even if I was probably givin' you flippin' head during it. Lord knows there wasn't anything happening on screen.

BRANDON: Aha, so you *do* remember!

BRITTANY: I JUST SAID I DID!

BRANDON: Name a movie Laurence Olivier was in. Any movie.

BRITTANY: You argue like the mentally ill, you know that?

BRANDON: Any movie. Literally any movie at all and I'll move on.

BRITTANY: *Sky Captain and the World of Tomorrow.*

BRANDON: You know what? I don't even wanna be in the same room with you anymore. First, you almost let Brady and Bennett get away, then you almost send a text message to all those flippin' idiots' phones when we were supposed to be radio silent that go round and now you're going to tell me the only movie you know with Laurence Olivier in it is the one where's he's fucking dead and they use archival footage?

BRITTANY: Language! What kind of relationship do you think this is?

BRANDON: Sorry. I'm good now. I'm fine. Just needed to rage a bit, babe.

BRITTANY: Yeah, I'll say. What time is it?

BRANDON: 11:50. Almost there.

BRITTANY: Do you think they heard us…communicating?

BRANDON: Nah. We've had worse fights next door to the kids and nothing.

BRITTANY: Kids hide disappointment in their parents pretty good. And that wasn't a fight; that was you trying to pigeonhole our generation with one movie from like thirty years ago. And I didn't almost let Brady and Bennett get away. They were pleading for their lives and I felt sorry for them. I had everything in hand. I figured let them get it out before they're dead. What's the flippin' harm in that?

BRANDON: We could have been caught!

BRITTANY: We're literally the least suspected couple here. Us? Working as a team? None of them suspected it, yeah? You said so yourself. What's with all the cold feet all of a sudden? We're almost done here. I don't know about you but I'm ready to hop in the jacuzzi right at 12:01. Yeah?

[Brittany goes to give Brandon a kiss off camera but he rebuffs it at the last second.]

BRANDON: Wait a minute. You said you didn't approve of their lifestyle.

BRITTANY: Who?

BRANDON: Brady and Bennett. You said those words.

BRITTANY: I said I didn't approve of them together. As a couple. We didn't even know they were gay in high school, babe.

BRANDON: You mean you let them beg for their lives while all the while you were thinking they sucked as a couple overall?

BRITTANY: Language, babe! I mean, yeah. They seemed kinda forced as a couple to me.

BRANDON: Forced? We haven't seen them in almost thirty years and they seemed forced?

BRITTANY: Yeah, like they were on edge and not happy or something. Maybe it was an abusive relationship?

BRANDON: They were probably just nervous to be around us as their true selves. What the heck are you talking about? Abusive? We just unalived the crap out of them and you're worried one of them might have been smacking around the other one a little bit?

BRITTANY: You're treading thin ice with your language, buster. Besides, the other couples seemed kinda like us. You know…

BRANDON: Miserable.

BRITTANY: You didn't even hesitate.

BRANDON: Comfortably numb.

BRITTANY: That's better, I guess. You know, you really—

[Rushed footsteps make their way to their room. Brittany turns the camera to the door just in time to see Tom and Abby Shelton rush in, covered in blood and sweat. They see the bodies of Callie and Micah. A look of horrific realization creeps across their faces as they stare down Brittany and Brandon.]

TOM SHELTON: It's you. You're both—

ABBY SHELTON: You miserable fucking pieces of—

[Brandon instantly shoots them both dead, emptying the entire clip of his 9mm Glock into them.

Brittany keeps the phone trained on their bodies. Several long seconds of silence takes over. Brittany moves the camera over to Brandon who scratches his head with his gun, completely nonplussed.]

BRITTANY: Well that's just great! All that plotting and planning and pretending to miss these assholes not to mention saving and scrimping to rent this overpriced Airbnb tourist trap only to kill the very last couple on New Year's Eve at 11:55 pm Eastern? What the fuck, Brandon?!

BRANDON: Babe, language! You're gonna make me blush over here. And what did you want me to do? Tell them a knock-knock joke? Sammy's real good at those. Do you think we should have Facetimed our six-year-old to see if he had a good knock-knock joke for the dillweed trainwreck couple who stole senior prom king and queen from us? I'm sure that woulda gone over real well.

[Brandon reloads his gun as Brittany continues talking]

BRITTANY: You could have stalled! Something. Anything. You had no problem improvising just a moment ago on *my* camera of all things. You couldn't have just faked it for five damn minutes? We were so close! I don't even feel like a jacuzzi anymore. Jacuzzi vibes gone.

BRANDON: We can just pretend. No one will know. This is for us, anyway.

BRITTANY: I'll know. And so will you. The only people who know will flippin' know. Jesus, Brandon. I thought you of all people would understand. And why are you reloading?

BRANDON: In case one of them's still alive. Don't you remember that movie *Scream?* The killer always comes back for one more how-do you-do. And that's beside the point; there you go getting all familiar with the Lord again. And you're telling me I should watch *my* language over here. Helloooo!

BRITTANY: I just wanted this one thing. You asked me what I wanted for Christmas and this is what I wanted. Do you not remember? I wanted it so bad I told you *last* Christmas so we could plan this right! Oh man, you could have had the best sex of your life but you just screwed it up like you screw everything else up. Five minutes. Five frickin' minutes was all we had left. I'm not even wet anymore. I was so close. You were gonna get the adult film star experience of a lifetime. You were so close. But now? You'll be lucky if I give you a fully clothed, low effort lap dance while you're blindfolded next weekend.

BRANDON: Wait a minute. Are you recording all of this?

BRITTANY: What? No, I—

BRANDON: You are! You recorded everything from when you took the camera back. And I'm the screwup? All we had to do is keep it off after I did my bit. But no, that wasn't good enough for you! You had to make sure your stamp was on it. Do you know what that feels like? To be the spare parent? To say or do something and have it countermanded almost instantly? It makes you feel like less than nothing. What am I even doing here? Twenty-seven years together and I don't even know anymore. You always complain I'm the fun one.

Dads are supposed to be the fun ones. Well guess what? I don't want to be the fun one! You can be the fun one for a change. I want to be the responsible one. How's *that* for a flippin' change? Maybe then I can go behind you and tell the kids something entirely different than what you said initially so we can both look like assholes. Does that sound like a good time to you? You getting jacuzzi vibes yet, babe?

BRITTANY: I hope you enjoyed that. I really hope that made you feel good. You have no idea what it's like to be the boring one. The humorless one. I'm *fun*. I know I am. I know you know that too. That's why you fell in love with me. We're both fun. But when it's time to grow up and take care of others sometimes that falls by the wayside. It's not a competition, Brandon. But I'm glad I know how you really feel. Maybe next Christmas we can buy each other couples counseling again. That'll really fix everything.

BRANDON: I'd rather be on that wife swap show. Maybe then I can see for sure if this is a normal relationship or not.

[Brittany pulls out a knife concealed in her sweater's front pocket. The kind where you can put both your hands inside for warmth and comfort. Blood still on it from killing their classmates.]

BRANDON: And what are you gonna do with that? Blowjobs don't require sharp objects. That kinda defeats the whole purpose.

BRITTANY: I'll defeat *your* purpose!

[Brittany lunges for Brandon with her knife, striking out and slicing him in his arm, causing him to drop his gun as a gout of red splashes out from the knife slash.]

BRANDON: Ah! Babe, what the hell—

BRITTANY: Language!

[She stabs at him again, taking a piece out of his stomach and sending him to the floor holding his midsection. Before he can even breathe again, she goes to attack once more. Without even thinking, he grabs the gun next to him and shoots her in the leg.]

BRITTANY: I can't believe you just shot me. That flippin' hurts!

BRANDON: You can swear now, it's an appropriate time to do so!

BRITTANY: I will after this separation goes through!

[She jumps at him, knife headed straight for his neck. She drops the phone and it lands at an angle, resting partially on Brandon's phone, still capturing everything. He fires as she's in midair and hits her in the chest. A kiss of blood spatters his cheek as her knife finds a resting place in his neck. They topple over in a heap, labored breathing filling the room and a pool of their blood enlarging around them.

Brittany's phones goes off with an alarm notification. A stock sound clip of a crowd of people shouting, "HAPPY NEW

YEAR!" *repeats over and over as Brittany's phone vibrates repeatedly, just out of reach of their widening blood puddle.*

Brandon tries to mouth something to Brittany through the knife in his neck as bubbles of blood piff and poof out of his neck hole.]

BRITTANY: I know, babe… I… Flippin' love you tooooo…

BRANDON: Haffy… Ooo… Ear…

[Brandon goes for a kiss with his dying breath. Brittany goes in to meet his lips with hers as she softly tries to respond.]

BRITTANY: Happ… Oh… Shit… Forgot… To… Stop… Recordin—

[She falls completely on top of him as their bloody frames mix, chests no longer moving at all.

Brandon's phone continues to buzz and shout, "Happy New Year!" several more times until it goes into snooze mode.

After a few long moments, his phone rings again. The name on the caller ID says "Sammy Boy".

FIFTEEN FILMS THAT INSPIRED THE STORIES IN THIS BOOK

MIRACLE ON 34th STREET (1947)

SANTA CLAUS CONQUERS THE MARTIANS (1964)

BLACK CHRISTMAS (1974)

HALLOWEEN II (1981)

TRADING PLACES (1983)

GREMLINS (1984)

ERNEST SAVES CHRISTMAS (1988)

NOROI: THE CURSE (2005)

MURDER PARTY (2007)

LAKE MUNGO (2008)

THANKSKILLING (2008)

RARE EXPORTS: A CHRISTMAS TALE (2010)

SUBURBAN GOTHIC (2014)

THE EDITOR (2014)

BETTER WATCH OUT (AKA SAFE NEIGHBORHOOD) (2016)

AUTHOR'S NOTES

THE TURKEY TROTS

Just an appeteaser for what's to come in this here book. I couldn't stop thinking about the yuppie neighbor couple from *National Lampoon's Christmas Vacation* and what it would be like if they were in their own boneheaded story. This is spiritually similar in tone to my story "It Was Probably Just the Wind" in my collection *The Comfy-Cozy Nihilist: A Handbook of Dark Fiction*. Also, the idea of Dwight D. Eisenhower avenging the sanctity of Thanksgiving like a Jedi promoting abstinence or something makes me laugh something fierce.

YUL BRYNNER'S YULETIDE POSSESSION SPECTACULAR

Lost and cursed film lore is my absolute jam. You got a movie about that kind of stuff? I'm there sight unseen. Books even more so. I think the epistolary/found footage route works wonderfully for haunted movie tropes. I'm also obsessed with movie stars and character actors from the 60s and 70s. Lee Van Cleef, Lee Marvin, William Holden, Ernest Borgnine, Charles Bronson, Steve McQueen, James Mason, and yes Yul Brynner. I could name a hundred more but I think you get the idea. Before the internet as we know it and before IMDb I had an encyclopedic knowledge of actors and their film credits. There's a stack of notebooks somewhere to prove it. Anyway, this story was originally published in *The Colour Out of Deathlehem* for Grinning Skull Press in 2021. It's also a bit of a primer for a novella I'm working on called *Method Hack*. Stay tuned for that one.

GOD REST YE SCARY SANTAMEN

Hallmark movies amaze and terrify me all at once. They make so many of them and they're such a reliable source of income for scores of actors and screenwriters (at least I think so) that it kind of boggles the mind. There's a formula for those films and I'm in awe of it all. That's where my idea for this story comes in. Like "The Shadow Over Innsmouth" but with less racism and more weresantas all in a tongue-in-cheek family holiday movie bow. Just the name Jingle Beach makes me giggle uncontrollably. This was also my first attempt at writing a gay couple as main characters in a story and I think it worked out well. You might very well disagree and I'd like to hear your thoughts if so. Seriously. This one originally appeared in *Santa Claws is Coming to Deathlehem* from Grinning Skull Press and was the first story ever published and got the ball rolling for me with this whole writing farce.

(PWB) PLEASE WRITE BACK

There's a lot going on with this one and I'm not going to reveal all of it to you as some of it is too personal to share in my opinion. But the kernel of an idea in the form of Santa being trapped in a closet at the toy factory in the North Pole frantically writing letters to kids in hopes they'll save him from some unspeakable otherworldly blight stuck with me for several years. The decision to make it epistolary came at the last minute and it's one of my sentimental favorite stories I've written so far. The whole thing with the little girl's uncle letting her watch Chuck Norris movies is somewhat true as my Aunt Kathy, my mom's oldest sister, had a whole entertainment center full of VHS tapes in the 90s that she would let me borrow. Chuck Norris, Steven Seagal, Wes Craven, John Carpenter. The good stuff, baby. She died in 2023 and I'd be lying if I said this story didn't make me think about her a whole hell of a lot more than I normally do. I don't think I ever returned her copy of Charlie Sheen's *Last of the Finest* and it haunts me to this day.

PART & PARCEL

Some of this is autobiographical. If not in actuality then it is autobiographical in a psychological and emotional nature. Does that make sense? No? Well then the part where I got punched in the face by my wife never happened but I did get trapped in a liminal space waiting for a seasonal job interview years ago and that was the real impetus for this story. Also, eating until you feel like you're going to literally explode at a few Thanksgiving meals didn't hurt as far as inspirational material goes. Parse what you want from the rest of the details within this yarn if you wish. Not telling you more anyways. Tee hee. Originally published in *Twas the Fright Before Christmas in Deathlehem* by Grinning Skull Press, this story finished off my my three-year-long streak of publishing Xmas stories with GSP. Not a bad run if I do say so myself. The real challenge with this one was coming up with a monster/entity that didn't involve Santa or the usual suspects. I decided upon Frau Perchta and I'm so glad I did. Look her up when you have a chance. She's a good egg.

AULD LANG STAB

I've had the idea of doing a "horrible couples at New Year's Eve" deal for a little while now and the chance to end this collection with such a thing felt so darn right. I had this whole backstory for six couples of all different backgrounds who all graduated from the same high school and were all invited to an exclusive grad couples only NYE party where the bodies drop in twos every hour on the hour. I'm not a huge fan of slashers in general (unless they take a darkly comic and/or absurd route) so I felt like starting at the end where the killers are revealed right away would be a fun and memorable exercise in found footage storytelling. Having them be a disgruntled married couple who've seen it all and want to literally kill monogamy and marital longevity makes me snort Pepsi out of my nose even when I'm not drinking Pepsi. Dialogue is my favorite thing to write and this one is just me going hog wild in that department. And for the record, I love *The Blair Witch Project*, even if Brittany does not.

ACKNOWLEDGMENTS

Thank you to Grinning Skull Press for originally publishing three of the Christmas stories collected here: "God Rest Ye Scary Santamen", "Yul Brynner's Yuletide Possession Spectacular", and "Part & Parcel". They published "God Rest Ye Scary Santamen" in 2020 and it was my first published story ever and inspired me to "always be keep going". I'm indebted to them for the duration.

Special thanks to Chad Farmer, Evan Baughfman, Paul Grammatico, and Mike Lombardo for providing valuable feedback for more than a few of the stories in this book. Their talent and consideration mean the world to me.

Thanks once more to the effervescent scion of holiday horror himself, Mike Lombardo, for the fantastic foreword to this collection and to Matthew Revert for the gobsmackingly awesome cover design as well as Matthew Wildasin for the fantabulous interior formatting.

And, as always, thanks to the readers, reviewers, cover artists, and editors who put in countless hours spreading the word about indie horror and genre fiction. This includes but is not limited to such luminaries as Christina Pfeiffer, Diana Richie, Milt Theodossiou, Dakota Dawe, A.A. Medina, Justin T. Coons, Tasha Scheidel, Robb Basham, Robb Carter, Erica Wetzel-Fields, and so very many others. You all rock so damn hard.

ABOUT THE AUTHOR

Nathan is an award-winning screenwriter, beloved film fest founder, decent producer, mediocre director, and an author of books with words in them.

His word work so far includes the grindhouse novel *Love Potion #666* as well as the short story collection *The Comfy-Cozy Nihilist: A Handbook of Dark Fiction*, both from GenreBlast Books. Upcoming releases include the novel *The Resurrection Girl*, plus novellas *Method Hack* and *Sacrificial Wolves*, as well as a second short story collection called *Misanthropy For Dummies*.

He runs the GenreBlast Film Festival, a Top 50 Genre Fest in the World, according to MovieMaker Magazine.

Nathan has co-directed a handful of short films with Chad Farmer as well as co-written a few books with him, including *Midnight Maniacs Volume 1* and *After Dark in Crazy Town*.

He's also the writer and producer of features films such as *Worst Laid Plans, Dead Format, Trucksquatch*, and *Terrors at the Drive-In*.

He lives just outside of Richmond, VA with his wife Mary and their two daughters. He loves independent pro-wrestling, Warren Zevon, Asian cinema, and a good spicy ramen.

Check out the Reel '96 Podcast, where he does a deep dive into every movie released in 1996. It sure is something and is available wherever halfway decent podcasts are available.

Find him on X and Instagram as @loogenhausen. On TikTok he lurks in the shadows as nathan.d.ludwig.

ABOUT THE PUBLISHER

GenreBlast Books is a small press started by Nathan D. Ludwig and Chad Farmer to highlight cross-genre fare that brings out the best in the weird, the unique, the horrific, the transgressive, and the darkly humorous.

Contact: genreblastbooks@gmail.com

Social Media: @genreblastbooks & @genreblast

www.genreblastbooks.com